BIGGLES AIR DETECTIVE

BIGGLES
AIR DETECTIVE

by
CAPT. W. E. JOHNS

PRINTED IN · GREAT BRITAIN
DEAN & SON Ltd.
32/54 Southwark St. · LONDON SE1 1UA
TRADE MARK

MADE AND PRINTED IN GREAT BRITAIN BY PURNELL AND SONS LTD.
PAULTON (SOMERSET) AND LONDON

603 03410 1

CONTENTS

THE CASE OF THE BLACK SHEEP

As Detective Air-Inspector Bigglesworth, better known as "Biggles", entered the office of the chief of his department, Air Commodore Raymond, Assistant Commissioner of New Scotland Yard, waved him to a chair and at the same time introduced a black-coated gentleman with whom he had been in conversation.

"Bigglesworth, this is Mr. Videll, Liaison Officer between the Board of Trade and His Majesty's Office of Customs and Excise," he said. "He has come here hoping that—well, if we can't give him any information you might give him the benefit of your expert opinion."

Biggles sat down. "What's the trouble?"

Mr. Videll answered. "The trouble, in a word, is nylons."

Biggles looked incredulous. "Nylons? Do you mean women's stockings?"

"Yes."

Biggles threw at his Chief a glance in which indignation and reproach were present. "For heaven's sake!" he exclaimed. "Don't tell me that we're expected to——"

The Air Commodore held up a hand. "Don't

jump to conclusions. Hear what Mr. Videll has to say. Nylons may be bigger business than you suppose. Go ahead, Videll."

The Liaison Officer explained. "We're worried by a serious leakage through our Customs barriers. American nylons are coming into this country in numbers far beyond the official quota. They're affecting the home market. The hosiery trade is complaining, and we've got to stop it."

"What are a few pairs of stockings, more or less?" murmured Biggles, looking slightly amused.

"Somebody is making a packet of money out of them, anyway," asserted Mr. Videll with asperity. "We're wondering if they're being smuggled in by aircraft. That's why I'm here."

"But surely if anyone was going seriously into the smuggling racket they'd choose a more profitable line than stockings," opined Biggles. "I doubt if an aircraft capable of doing the transatlantic run could be operated to make a profit out of them. Can you give me any figures? What do nylons weigh?"

"A pair of real Du Pont Crystal nylon stockings weigh less than half an ounce," stated the Liaison Officer. "Say three pairs to an ounce, or forty-eight pairs to a pound. A parcel weighing a mere fifty pounds would contain two thousand pairs of hose. They could probably be bought in America, wholesale for less than ten shillings a pair. Here, they are retailing in the black market at anything from twenty-five to thirty shillings a pair, which means that a fifty-pound parcel would show a profit of something in the order of £2,000. Work that out in quantities and you'll see that nylons are by no means mere chicken-feed."

"You surprise me," admitted Biggles. "Are you sure the stuff isn't trickling through in the kit-bags of foreign merchant sailors?"

"A number were being brought in that way at one time, but since we got the big stick out it has pretty well dried up. No, these consignments are coming through in bulk. While they last they nearly flood the market. Then there's a gap until the next consignment arrives. That's been happening at the rate of four times a year for the past twenty months."

"And you've no clue as to how this racket is being worked?"

"We thought we had, but somehow we can't make it fit. Intensive investigation revealed that the appearance of the nylons invariably coincided with the arrival of a certain cargo boat—the *Sirocco*—which, flying the Panama flag, takes the north route to Liverpool. It must have been coincidence, because the last time the *Sirocco* came in we were waiting for her. We searched the ship and every man on her—and that's a job we know how to do. The nylons weren't there. We checked every parcel leaving the dock, yet within a couple of days a fresh lot of nylons were on sale in the London black market."

Biggles took a cigarette from his case and tapped it thoughtfully on the back of his hand before lighting it. "Hm! Coincidence is always interesting. In my experience there's usually something more to it than just coincidence. Where's the *Sirocco* now?"

"Two hundred miles out in the Atlantic, heading for Liverpool."

"Which means that you're expecting another load of nylons to arrive pretty soon?"

Mr. Videll shrugged. "Another consignment is about due, but I don't see how the *Sirocco* can have anything to do with it. Personally, I believe the stuff is being flown over, but I couldn't guess how."

Biggles shook his head. "I doubt it."

"Why?"

"To start with, we're watching the sky pretty closely. Of course, I couldn't swear that there isn't an unlicensed machine about, but I'm pretty sure it couldn't operate regularly without being spotted sooner or later. Apart from that, it's a matter of simple mathematics. I doubt if it would be possible to operate an aircraft, capable of crossing the Atlantic, for the sole purpose of importing nylons— I mean, to show a profit and make the risks worth while. Aircraft are expensive toys. Or put it this way. If such a machine was operating the pilot would choose a more profitable line of goods than nylons. Again, if an aircraft was being used surely the nylons would arrive in a steady stream instead of only four times a year. That's the rate of a tramp steamer. An aircraft could easily make the trip forty times in the same period. Then, what about petrol? You can't buy petrol by the thousand gallons without somebody getting inquisitive." Biggles looked at the Air Commodore. "That's my opinion, sir, but we can go into the thing more closely if you like."

"I wish you would—just covering the air angle, of course," answered the Air Commodore.

Biggles got up. "Very well, sir." He turned to the Liaison Officer. "If aviation does come into this, it shouldn't take us long to pick up the scent. I'll get cracking on it right away." He left the room and returned to his own office, where Air Constable Ginger Hebblethwaite was on duty. "What's the weather report for sea area Rockall, Malin and the North Channel?" he asked.

Ginger went over to a flag-labelled map that covered most of one wall. "Fine and warm. Wind moderate, north to north-east. Sea calm. Conditions likely to persist."

"Good enough," returned Biggles. "Get your hat. We're going to have a look at it. I aim to be there about dawn. I'll tell you why on the way."

"That looks like her."
The speaker was Ginger, and he spoke from the

second pilot's seat of an Air Police Service Saro amphibian, which, as indicated by the instruments, was cruising on a westerly course at an altitude of a thousand feet.

Biggles was at the controls. Dawn was just breaking. Below lay the Atlantic, cold, dreary and monotonous, in the half light, rolling away to the edge of the world on all sides except to the east, where dark smudges marked the coastlines of Northern Ireland and the Western Isles of Scotland. In all that vast expanse of ocean only two ships could be seen. Far to the north a destroyer was outward bound on the King's business. Several miles to the south a typical salt-water tramp was ploughing her way westward with a wisp of grimy smoke hanging like a feather from her funnel. Behind her, as far as the eye could see but fading in the distance, was her track, a broad line of oily water sprinkled at intervals with garbage.

"Yes, that must be the *Sirocco*," said Biggles. "Keep your eyes skinned. I'm going to back-track her." He altered his course slightly, and throttled back, losing a little height.

Ginger, with powerful binoculars to his eyes, studied the track, as Biggles, still heading seaward, took up a course a little to the right of it.

It was ten minutes before Ginger spoke. "I can see something I can't identify," he reported. "Go down a bit."

The aircraft slipped off more height.

"Looks as if it might be a barrel, painted orange on top, with a black cross," went on Ginger. "It might be a mine."

"We'll have a look at it," decided Biggles. "Watch the sky now; I don't want anyone to arrive while we're on the surface." He cut the engine, and air sang over the planes as he side-slipped steeply towards his objective. In five minutes he had landed beside it.

"All clear topsides," announced Ginger.

Biggles taxied to the object that had engaged their attention and, climbing out on a wing, examined it closely. Another minute and he was back in his seat. "Two motor tyres, inflated and lashed together to make flotation gear for an hermetically sealed tin box," he muttered. "I'd say that's what we're looking for. We shall soon know." The engine roared as he opened the throttle. The aircraft raced across the water, unstuck and climbed steeply. "It won't do to be seen," he went on. "Frankly, I reckoned we should find a fishing boat or a small yacht of some sort hanging about, but as there's nothing of the sort in sight it begins to look as if the rescue party will come the way we came. If I'm right it won't be long, either. In half an hour that track will have disappeared. Don't take your eyes off the mark." Not until the altimeter registered ten thousand feet did he level out and begin a wide circle.

Five minutes passed. Then, "Tally-ho!" he called sharply. "Here he comes."

Ginger looked round and, following the direction of Biggle's eyes, saw what appeared to be a white water-beetle skimming low over the water, following the wake of the steamer. He turned his glasses on it. "Moth seaplane," he reported.

"Not many of that type about," murmured Biggles. "It shouldn't take us long to trace the owner from the Civil Register. Ah-ha! He's going down."

"If he looks up he'll spot us," warned Ginger.

Biggles smiled grimly. "I'd wager the last thing he suspects is that he's being watched. It doesn't matter, anyway. He couldn't shake us off if he tried."

There was no more talking. Together they watched the seaplane taxi to the orange object. The pilot climbed out on a float, and presently the two tyres were seen floating away. The box was put in the back seat of the machine, which then took off again and headed in the direction from which it had come.

Biggles, maintaining his height, followed. The distant coasts hardened. Hills appeared. For a little while it looked as if the Moth might be making for Northern Ireland, but at the finish it swung round towards the many islands that stand like sentinals along the west coast of Scotland.

"Get your chart handy," ordered Biggles.

Ginger unfolded an Admiralty chart on his knees.

"He's going in," said Biggles, his eyes still on the Moth. "He seems to be making for that longish island with a piece bitten out of the middle."

"I've got it," announced Ginger. "The name is Lagganmalloch Island."

"Good! For the moment that's all we want to know," returned Biggles. "That name rings a bell in my memory. I believe the island was a temporary marine aircraft base for submarine-spotting during the war. No doubt it has since been abandoned." He turned away. "We'll run home and see what the records have to tell us."

Three hours later, in his office at the Yard, with Ginger watching, Biggles was turning over the pages of the official Register of Civil Aircraft and private landing-grounds, to which he had added his own notes. It did not take him long to find what he was looking for. "Here we are," he said. "Lagganmalloch. Temporary Service Seaplane Base, now relinquished. Island bought in 1946 by Flight-Lieutenant R. Q. Paullson, D.F.C., for farming. Specialises in black St. Kilda sheep. Applied for private owner's licence as communications between island and mainland bad, and impossible sometimes in winter. MacRowdens coastal steamer service calls weekly, Wednesdays at three-thirty, for mail and freight. Licence granted. Type, Moth seaplane. Maker's number R.1247. Wool is shipped to Louis Vanberger & Co., Glasgow, via Baltroonie. That's all." Biggles sighed, closed the book, looked up and shook his head sadly.

"What a fool Paullson must be to think he could get away with that, although no doubt the idea must have looked all right. Apparently the black sheep didn't pay. Pity. Stout pilot, Paullson. I remember meeting him once. But there, I suppose of the tens of thousands of war-trained pilots it was inevitable that one or two of them should strike hard times and go off the rails."

"He'll go to gaol for this," observed Ginger moodily. "The thing must have seemed easy. One sailor on board the *Sirocco*, to toss the consignment overboard at a prearranged spot, was all that was necessary. All Paullson had to do was back-trail the steamer and pick it up. Do you suppose he flies the stuff to the mainland?"

"He wouldn't be quite such a fool as that," opined Biggles. "Besides, there'd be no need. It would be easier, and less risky, to slip it into some of the stuff he exports, a bale of wool, for instance. There would be no Customs check at Baltroonie on inter-island traffic. I imagine someone collects the stuff there and sends it on to London. I've got a feeling Paullson didn't organise this himself. There would be difficulties at the American end. I'd say there's a professional crook in it. If so, he's the real sand in the gear-box."

"Yes," muttered Ginger. "He'll have his bolt-hole ready too, no doubt. When the showdown comes he'll get away with it and leave Paullson to take the rap."

"Probably." Biggles drummed on the table with his fingers. "I think we'll make sure of our facts before we go any further. I'm going to slip back and have a word with Paullson. It may save us, and him, a lot of trouble. I'm convinced he isn't really a bad hat—but, if he goes to gaol, he will be when he comes out."

A few hours later, with the sun past its zenith, Biggles landed in the little sheltered bay which during the war had been used as a marine aircraft reconnaissance base. Signs of this were still in evidence. There was a slipway, with a hanger behind it, near an old wooden pier on which was waiting, ready for the weekly steamer now approaching, island produce, which included live sheep, cases of eggs, and some bales—presumably wool. Here also the population of the island had forgathered to collect their mail, newspapers and the like.

Biggles ran up the slipway, made fast, and,

followed by Ginger, went ashore under the curious eyes of the little group of spectators. Taking no notice of these, they made their way to the merchandise and examined the labels. Biggles paid particular attention to the bales of wool. All were consigned to Louis Vanberger & Co., Glasgow. With one exception all the labels were printed. The exception was an orange-coloured label on which the address had been written. "This will be the one," he murmured softly.

By this time a tallish, good-looking young man of about twenty-six, in home-spun tweeds, had separated himself from the spectators and was walking towards them. He was slightly pale, Ginger noted, and his forehead was knit in a worried frown—which supported Biggles's belief that, assuming it was Paullson, he was not an habitual lawbreaker.

"Are you looking for something?" asked the man sharply.

Biggles considered him without hostility. "You're Paullson, aren't you?"

"I am," was the curt reply. "Who are you?"

"Detective Air-Inspector Bigglesworth of Scotland Yard," answered Biggles quietly. "I'd like a word with you in private."

The ex-officer's face turned ashen. He appeared to have difficulty in speaking. "Come over to my house, it isn't far," he managed to get out.

They walked the few hundred yards to the house in silence. Paullson went to a sideboard and with a shaking hand poured himself a stiff drink. "Have one?" he offered.

"I don't use it, thanks," replied Biggles. "I needn't tell you why I'm here," he went on. "My advice to you is to come clean. It may make things easier for you and it'll save time."

Paullson moistened his lips. "What do you want to know?" he asked in a low voice. "Speak quietly; my mother's in the house."

Biggles went on. "This morning, shortly after daybreak, at a point roughly ninety miles south-west of here, you landed in the track of a ship named *Sirocco* and picked up a parcel."

"Who says so?" demanded Paullson, with a feeble attempt at bluster.

"I say so," answered Biggles evenly. "I was watching you. Am I right?"

"Yes." Paullson's voice was hardly audible.

"What was in the parcel?"

"Cigarettes."

Biggles looked hard at the man. "Who told you so?"

"The man to whom I forwarded the parcel."

"Have you ever opened one of these parcels? This, I believe, is the seventh."

"No."

"You took the man's word for it?"

"Of course."

"What did he pay you for doing this?"

"Pay? He didn't pay me anything."

"Don't ask me to believe that you did it for nothing?" Biggles voice was sarcastic.

"No. He sends me some of the cigarettes. I like American cigarettes. We don't get many English cigarettes over here, anyway. My nerves are not too good and I smoke a lot."

"I see," said Biggles slowly. "You knew, of course, that such a practice was highly irregular, to say the least of it?"

"Yes, I knew that," admitted Paullson frankly. "I took a chance."

"And the parcel you picked up this morning is now in a bale of wool addressed to Vanberger & Co.?"

Paullson hesitated. "Yes," he admitted.

"Was it to do this that you bought an aircraft?"

Paullson frowned. "Good lor, no! An aircraft is the only reasonable means of getting to and fro to the mainland."

"Tell me, then: how did this business start?" asked Biggles.

"I send my fleeces to Vanberger," explained Paullson. "He knew I had an aircraft. He came here to see me on business. I happened to be out of cigarettes and he said he could get me plenty, if I would help. That's really all there was to it."

"I am afraid there was more to it than that," said Biggles seriously. "Those parcels contained contraband to the tune of £2,000 a time."

Paullson dropped into a chair, lips apart, eyes wide. "The crook," he breathed heavily. "I'll go and withdraw that last consignment."

"Nothing of the sort," Biggles told him. "Let it go. I imagine Vanberger will be at Baltroonie to collect it."

"You're asking me to give him away," protested Paullson.

"Listen to me," said Biggles earnestly. "Somebody is going to gaol over this business. If Vanberger has his way, it'll be you. If you've any sense it'll be him. You've one chance to save yourself, and because I believe your version I'm going to give you that chance. You've got to turn King's Evidence. You needn't be squeamish about it because Vanberger has no interest in you and he's played the dirty on you all along."

Paullson buried his face in his hands. "This will about kill my mother when she hears of it."

"You might have thought of that earlier."

"All right," agreed Paullson wearily. "What else do you want to know?"

"What times does the island steamer discharge cargo at Baltroonie?"

"Half-past eight tomorrow morning."

"Good. Then we've plenty of time. What's the name of the man on the *Sirocco* who throws the stuff overboard?"

"I've no idea. I wasn't interested. I only know that after the ship has docked he goes to Vanberger for payment."

"And that's all you can tell me?"

"That's all I know. I must have been crazy."

"You were. Will you give me your word that you won't be such a fool again?"

"I've had my lesson," said Paullson bitterly. "If ever I get my hands on that lying crook Vanberger I'll knock his block off."

"It's unlikely that you'll get your hands on him because, unless I've missed my guess, he'll be going somewhere where you won't be able to get to him. I'll be moving along now. You stay here until you hear from me again. One last word of advice. Lay off that bottle. The stuff's expensive, and it makes neither for clear thinking nor good flying. So long. Come on, Ginger."

By the time they were at the water-front the steamer, having picked up its freight, was on its way. A minute or two later Biggles passed over it as he set a course for the mainland.

"Make a signal to the Chief," he told Ginger. "Ask him to have Mr. Videll in the office at seven o'clock this evening. You can say I have news for him."

"Okay." Ginger turned on the radio transmitter.

At five minutes to seven, when they walked into the Air Commodore's office, Mr. Videll was already there.

"What's the news?" he asked eagerly. "My word! You move fast."

"That's what aeroplanes are for," Biggles told him, smiling.

"I'm all agog to hear what you've discovered."

Biggles answered: "At eight-thirty tomorrow morning one of MacRowden's regular service Scottish west coast steamers will put into Baltroonie to handle freight and passengers. In her cargo are several bales of wool—fleeces of black wool. One has a plain yellow label. In it, wrapped in the wool, you'll find your next consignment of nylons."

Mr. Videll stared. "Are you pulling my leg?"

"No. I'm too tired to play games. I've travelled quite a few miles since I last saw you."

"Do you know to whom this wool is consigned?"

"A Glasgow firm named Louis Vanberger & Co."

"How did the nylons get in the wool—can you tell me that?"

"I can. They were put in by a man who didn't know what was in the parcel," said Biggles. "I've satisfied myself of that. The man you want is

Vanberger—or the man who handles his stuff. You can pick him up at Baltroonie with the goods on him, or you can let him go and check up on the addresses of all the parcels he sends out during the next few days. That should provide you with a list of his distributing agents in London. You could then get the whole bunch in the bag together. Incidentally, you were on the right track with the *Sirocco*. A member of the crew brings the stuff over from America. He goes to Vanberger's office for the pay-off. If you watch the crew of the ship, and Vanberger's office, you should get your man."

The Air Commodore was smiling at the expression on the face of the Liaison Officer, who naturally wanted to know how all this information had been gathered in so short a time.

"That's a trade secret," chaffed Biggles.

"But how on earth did the nylons get into a bale of wool on board an island steamer?" cried Mr. Videll.

"The earth had nothing to do with it," Biggles told him. "The trick was worked partly by water and partly by air. Of course, the skipper of the steamer has no idea of what he's carrying; and, as I told you, the man who put the parcel on board didn't know what was in it. He was merely the dupe of some smart guys. I've had a word with him and he's ready to turn King's Evidence, which should be all you need to send the real crooks to where they can't get into mischief for a long while. So I hope you'll be able to fix things to let him off with a caution, even if you have to summons him—which I hope you won't. He's had his lesson; it's shaken him pretty badly, and he's given me his word that the thing won't happen again."

The Air Commodore put in a word. "All the same, hadn't we better cancel his pilot's licence to make sure?"

"No," answered Biggles. "He did a good job in the last war. If there's another, we shall need him, so he might as well keep his hand in. Moreover, he's maintaining a little establishment that we may be glad to use on some occasion."

"All right, if you say so," agreed the Air Commodore. He turned to the Board of Trade official. "That, Mr. Videll, should be as much as you need to know."

The official got up. "Yes, and a thousand thanks. We can handle the rest of the case ourselves." He sighed. "It looks as if nylons are going to be in short supply again."

Biggles opened the door for him. "There shouldn't be as many about as there were, even in the black market."

Mr. Videll hesitated. "As a matter of detail, what is the line of business of this fellow whom Vanberger got to do his dirty work?"

"Sheep," answered Biggles smiling. "Black sheep."

"How very appropriate."

"But he isn't one of them."

"I'll take your word for it," promised Mr. Videll as he closed the door.

THE CASE OF THE VISITING SULTAN

Biggles jumped down from the cockpit of an Auster aircraft which he had just been testing. "She's still inclined to fly a bit left wing low," he told Flight-Sergeant Smyth, who came forward from where he had been watching.

"I'll attend to it, sir," promised the Flight-Sergeant. "Air Commodore Raymond is waiting for you in the Ops Room."

Biggles walked on, pulling off his gloves. Entering the Operations Room, he threw them, with his cap, into a chair and turned to the Air Commodore, who, with a worried expression on his face and hands thrust deep into trousers pockets, stood waiting.

"'Morning, sir," greeted Biggles cheerfully. "Or is it a good morning?" he added softly.

"Is there any question about it?" inquired the Air Commodore irritably.

"From your expression I'd say you're not interested in the weather, anyhow," murmured Biggles.

"Quite right, I'm not," was the curt rejoinder.

Biggles sighed, reached for a cigarette, lit it and dropped into a chair. "Some people say that the best thing to do with a spot of bother is to pass it on to someone else," he suggested. "If you agree, go right ahead. I'm listening."

The Air Commodore nodded gloomily. "Very well. If you read the newspapers you may have noticed an item to the effect that a native ruler named Oba I'Mobi, Sultan of Lashanti, in West Africa, is coming to London for the Colonial Conference."

"I didn't notice it, and, speaking personally, I couldn't care less," returned Biggles evenly.

"As is customary with native princes he insists on bringing with him his court regalia."

"And just what does that consist of?"

"Diamonds, mostly. Some of the best diamonds in the world are found in the gravel which comprises much of the Sultan's territory. Naturally, he has the pick. So did his forebears. The result is a collection of considerable size and perfect quality."

"Pretty to see, no doubt; but I wouldn't stand in a queue for a private view of them," averred Biggles. "What have they to do with me, anyway?"

"Nothing—yet; but they are giving me a headache," asserted the Air Commodore. "It happens that the Sultan, having been educated in this country, is a young man with progressive ideas, in which, being wealthy, he can indulge. Among other civilised conveniences he possesses an aircraft, a hanger, and a private airfield adjacent to his palace."

"Who flies the plane?"

"He does. He got a B Licence while he was over here."

"What's the machine?"

"An elderly photographic reconnaissance Mosquito which he bought from Disposals. In it he intends to fly himself and his young son to London."

"The machine has plenty of range and ought to be able to make the run non-stop," declared Biggles. "What's the worry? Are you afraid he'll lose his way?"

"If he did he would have himself to blame," answered the Air Commodore bitterly. "Until a few hours ago I was not in the least concerned. Unfortunately a factor has just arisen which has spoilt the appetites of those of us responsible for His Highness's safety. Did you ever hear of a man named Rocky Cordova?"

"The name rings a bell, but I can't place it."

"Rocky Cordova is America's number one bad man. For a long time now the Federal Police have tried in vain to get him by the pin-feathers. Like the Sultan he thinks on modern lines. Like the Sultan he is rich and lives in a palace surrounded by guards. Like the Sultan he employs a private aircraft for fast transportation. Again like the Sultan—and this is the real wasp in the jam—he collects diamonds. He boasts that he has the best collection in the United States, which may be true, since he has for years been taking them from their rightful owners. Hence the nickname Rocky—rocks being the crook's vernacular for diamonds."

Biggles shrugged. "All right. So Rocky collects rocks. I haven't any, so he won't improve his collection at my expense."

"This morning," went on the Air Commodore coldly, "my opposite number in New York rang up to give me the tip that Rocky has gone for a holiday —by air, of course. Through a stool-pigeon they know where he has gone, and it is not the sort of place a man would go for his health. Guess where."

Biggles smiled faintly. "The penny has dropped. My guess is West Africa."

"You've got it in one."

"And you've got a feeling that he may be aiming to get some bigger and better diamonds?"

"Can you think of any other reason why a man of his type should take a vacation so far from the high-spots in which he delights to swank?"

"No—unless he's made a quick getaway from the police."

"The police have nothing on him. So far he's always outsmarted them. We've got to see he doesn't outsmart us by lifting the Sultan's decorations."

"How's he going to do that—by breaking into the palace?"

"Not a hope. The place bristles with armed guards. If only the Sultan would stay there we should have nothing to worry about. If Rocky is on the job he'll make his grab between Lashanti and London."

"Have you any reason to suppose that he's on the job?"

"No, but his arrival in West Africa at this moment can hardly be coincidence. Rightly or wrongly, I'm bound to work on the assumption that Rocky is after the Sultan's rocks."

Biggles took another cigarette and tapped it thoughtfully. "What machine does Rocky fly?"

"A converted American war type; a single-engined, four-seat attack plane called the Cobra. At least, it's supposed to be converted, but there's reason to suspect that it still carries its armament. The Sultan's Mosquito is unarmed. The Cobra is slightly faster."

"Does Rocky fly himself?"

"No. He employs a Mexican ex-war pilot named Juan Laroula."

Biggles got up and studied a wall map of the world. "It's hard to see what Rocky can do once the Mosquito is off the ground," he opined. "If he shot the Mosquito down it might go up in flames, in which case I imagine the diamonds would be ruined?"

"He might not find it necessary to do that. He

might, by using his guns, force the Sultan to land. An unarmed pilot, suddenly attacked, would instinctively make for the ground."

"True enough," admitted Biggles. "But there's only one place where that could happen. For the first part of the run the Mosquito will be over sheer jungle where, if it crashed, Rocky couldn't get to it, anyway. The last half of the journey, assuming the Sultan takes the direct route, will be over water, and there would be no point in shooting him down in the drink. There's just one area where a landing might be made, and that's a place I should be sorry to choose myself. I mean the Spanish territory, Rio de Oro, which is mostly desert of the worst sort. A machine flying from Lashanti to London dead on its course would be over it for an hour or so. If Rocky intends to attack the Mosquito it will be there, because it would be pointless to force it down anywhere else." Biggles returned to his chair. "Where exactly is Rocky now?"

"I don't know," admitted the Air Commodore. "I haven't had time even to start enquiries. It would be a simple matter for him to slip over the African coast at night, or above the overcast if there was any cloud."

"And once in he could lie low for weeks if necessary, unless native rumour gave him away," observed Biggles. "There's no shortage of landing grounds. Scores of landing strips were put down from the West Coast to Egypt for American machines carrying war stores to the Middle East."

"Rocky's pilot, Laroula, was on that run for two years, so he should know all about them," muttered the Air Commodore. "We haven't time to search thousands of square miles of wild country."

"When does the Sultan leave for England?"

"A week today. Naturally he'll leave in the morning to do the trip in daylight."

"Would Rocky know that?"

"Unfortunately, not anticipating anything of this sort, the trip and the date were given publicly in the press. No doubt that's how Rocky knew about it."

"How about getting the Sultan to alter the date?"

"He couldn't without upsetting all his arrangements. Besides, what reason could we give? If we told him the truth I doubt if he'd believe it."

"Probably it wouldn't do any good, anyway," murmured Biggles. "If Rocky is as smart as they say, he'd anticipate such a move and be ready for it. I'd say he'll park himself somewhere along the route north of Lashanti. In that case he'd only have to wait for the Mosquito to come along."

"You're not helping me," complained the Air Commodore. "Can't you be a bit more constructive?"

"How about providing an R.A.F. escort all the way?" suggested Biggles.

The Air Commodore shook his head. "Even if

it were practicable, that wouldn't do. For one thing it would arouse the jealousy of other potentates who, not having an escort, would think the Sultan was being specially honoured. Again, we can't fly service planes over foreign territory without permission, and that would take more time than we have available."

Biggles shrugged a shoulder. "Well, what are you going to do? If there's anything I can do, tell me and I'll do it."

"I came to you as a practical pilot for a suggestion," declared the Air Commodore. "The Sultan won't change his plans. He's dead keen on attending the conference, and if we asked him not to come he might suspect a sinister reason, in which case we should lose his friendship."

"If he comes, and gets bumped off on the way, you'll lose his friendship, anyhow," Biggles pointed out grimly. He looked at the Air Commodore suspiciously. "I believe you've had an idea at the back of your mind all the time we've been talking."

"Well—er—yes. Matter of fact, I had, but I thought I'd explore all the possibilities before I broached it. Frankly, I thought you might fly out and form a sort of unofficial escort."

"I thought of that, but I didn't suggest it because I couldn't see what good it could do," answered Biggles. "I mean, I couldn't very well attack a machine on the mere suspicion that it was going to attack the Sultan; and if I waited for the attack to be made I should be too late to save the Mosquito. True, I might get Rocky, but that wouldn't help the Sultan if he had already been shot to bits. Just a minute, though." Biggles thought for a minute. "There may be one way out of the difficulty," he went on slowly. "Have we got a resident official in Lashanti?"

"Yes. Sir Milton Chambers, Governor of the colony."

"Would he co-operate with us?"

"Undoubtedly."

"All right. Then let us try the old Q-ship trick. If it came off it should give the Sultan a safe trip and might dispose of this dangerous crook at the same time. This is all you have to do. Ask Sir Milton to start a rumour that the Sultan has decided to start an hour earlier than he intended. Rocky will hear it and switch his time-table accordingly. Get me a Mosquito from the Air Ministry, complete with guns. I'll fly it out. On the morning of the flight I'll take off at the hour which, according to the rumour, the Sultan should leave the ground. I then head for home. If Rocky is on the job he'll come for me, supposing me to be the Sultan. We then settle the business between us. Whether he gets me, or I get him, the Sultan, starting an hour later, should get through without interference. How's that?"

The Air Commodore looked dubious. "According

to your theory, if you have to go down you'll be in the Rio de Oro. You'd never get out alive."

"I'll make provision for that by having Ginger waffle along behind me in another machine. If I go down he can pick me up—or at any rate he'd know exactly where I was. Don't worry about that angle. If the plan is okay with you I'll fix the details."

"Good enough," agreed the Air Commodore. "Where are you going to land when you get to the coast? You can't very well use the Sultan's airfield at Masdu."

"Is there anywhere else?"

"There's Kunali, the airfield the Sultan used before Masdu was cleared. There's no one there now. It's about twenty miles away."

"That should suit us," declared Biggles. "You might have some petrol sent there."

"All right. I'll come out with you and fix things up." The Air Commodore smiled bleakly. "It'd be funny if we were barking up the wrong tree all the time."

"It wouldn't be so funny if we were barking up the right one and did nothing about it," asserted Biggles.

On the morning of the seventh day following this conversation with the Air Commodore Biggles stood at the entrance of a dilapidated hangar on Kunali airfield, surveying without enthusiasm the arid airstrip and the jungle that surrounded it. When, presently, Ginger joined him, after a glance at the sky he remarked: "It looks like being another scorcher."

"Which means that the atmosphere over the desert sector is going to be more than somewhat choppy," observed Ginger.

"If we have nothing worse than bumps to deal with that'll suit me fine,"—averred Biggles.

"It'll be a silly sort of anti-climax if nothing happens after all," opined Ginger.

"It'll be the sort of anti-climax that I like," returned Biggles. "If Rocky shows up one of us is going to collide with something solid, and whether it's covered with jungle or sand won't make much difference. Keep well above and behind me— unless Rocky looks like getting away with it. According to the Air Commodore's information this chap Laroula is a good pilot. But there, Rocky wouldn't be likely to employ a nitwit. Here comes the Air Commodore now. I imagine he'll have the latest gen from the palace."

The Air Commodore, driving the Governor's car, pulled up and got out. "Are you all set?" he asked.

"Ready and waiting to see the back of this blistering hothouse," Biggles told him. "Have things gone all right at your end?"

"As right as I can make them," replied the Air Commodore. "The Sultan knows nothing about what's going on. As far as he's concerned everything is normal. He's taking off, with his son and his box of rocks, at nine o'clock; but according to the story circulated he'll be leaving the floor at eight. The rumour is pretty general by now, so Rocky should have heard it."

Biggles nodded. "That's fine. I'll move off at five minutes to eight, circle Masdu, and set a course for home. Ginger is coming along behind. If Rocky hasn't turned up by the time I reach Morocco I shall turn back and watch the Sultan until he has crossed the coast. After that he'll be safe. As there will then be nothing for me to do I shall probably look in at Gibraltar and refuel."

"That's about all we can do," said the Air Commodore. "See you later—I hope." He got back into his car and drove off.

Biggles looked at his watch. "We might as well get mobile," he told Ginger. "Don't follow me too closely. I shall grab some altitude between here and Masdu and then head due north. Let's go."

Ten minutes later Biggles's Mosquito raised a wall of dust as it sped across the airfield and into the air. The palace, and the native town near to which it stood, were soon in view. He did not actually fly over them, but, making a detour, picked up his course on the far side. At an altitude of five thousand feet he put the machine on even keel at cruising speed and settled down for the long run ahead.

Above, the sky was a dome of unbroken blue. Below, the scene was a monotonous expanse of forest stretching to the horizon, with a miasma of mist still hanging over the depressions. Here, he felt, there was nothing to fear, for a falling machine would disappear as utterly as a stone dropped in an ocean. Even so, he began a methodical scrutiny of the air around him, above and below, studying it closely section by section and paying particular attention to the glare that marked the position of the sun. Far above and behind, a tiny spot against the blue told him that Ginger was on the job.

For nearly three hours these conditions persisted. For this he was prepared. But when, far ahead, a line of what appeared to be burnished copper crept over the edge of the world his body stiffened slightly as his muscles braced themselves for swift action. The most notorious and least known of all deserts was at hand. Rio de Oro. River of Gold. Who had put the word river into the name of seventy-three thousand square miles of waterless desert he did not know; but it must, he thought, have been someone with a grim sense of humour. Any gold other than the superheated sand was likely to remain. So would an aircraft forced down in it. Yet if his reasoning had been correct it was here that the American crook and his Mexican pilot would make their bid for the Sultan's diamonds . . . if that was the purpose of their visit to Africa.

The area of gleaming sterility became broader as it drew nearer. The tropical forest that had for so long been passing below began at last to break down into little islands of scrub, sparse and sun-scorched, with odd trees, their feet in the yellow tide, wilting like tired sentinels.

Biggles stared long and steadfastly into the world of blue above him, to the east, and west, and the direction from which he had come. He could see nothing but the eternal blue, fading to steely grey where it met the horizon. Where was Rocky? He should soon show up if he was coming. He throttled back a trifle to give him an opportunity to overtake should he be coming along behind. The sooner the suspense was over the better, he decided.

Twenty minutes passed—long minutes they seemed to Biggles, whose nerves were keyed up, knowing that death might strike at any moment. Nothing happened, except that the aircraft began to rock in the heat-distorted air. The engines droned their tireless dirge. Above, the implacable sky remained unchanged. Below, the waste of sun-blasted rock and sand moved slowly past as more came into view.

It was a movement on the sand that told him that his vigil was at an end. A shadow, some distance to the right, caught his eye, a broad black mark where a moment before there had been none. He watched it and saw that it was moving, moving at the same pace as himself. That told him everything. He was no longer alone in the sky. Another machine was there, flying level with him, between him and the blazing orb of the sun. It could not, he knew, be Ginger, who would not depart from his orders to remain in the rear. With the sun now high, his shadow would be almost directly underneath him.

Pulling down his dark glasses that he wore for the purpose, Biggles altered his course slightly and, half closing his eyes, tried to probe the glare. It was not easy, but he caught a glimpse of a dark spot that seemed to be coming nearer. Instead of straining his eyes trying to follow it, he watched the shadow on the ground, knowing that from its movements he would be able to judge what the machine was doing.

Five minutes passed, a period during which the relative positions of himself and the shadow on the ground remained unchanged. What was Rocky doing? For what was he waiting? Then, glancing down, he understood. Below him was a chaos of broken rocks on which it would be impossible for a machine to land. Ahead was a reasonably flat plateau of sand. He smiled grimly. So Rocky was merely saving himself the trouble of having to walk some distance to his victim. The plateau would obviously suit him better.

Biggles, with his eyes never moving from the shadow, waited, and while he waited he found himself pondering on a situation outside his experience. It was more difficult than war flying, when the enemy is known, his machine marked, and is fair game to be attacked on sight when met. Here, the other machine could not be accounted an enemy until the pilot had enjoyed the advantage of striking the first blow—a blow that might prove fatal. This waiting to be struck before he dare strike back was more than distasteful, particularly as Biggles was anxious to get the business finished. But he could do nothing until the other man had made the first move.

He tried to think of some way to force the issue, but the only plan he could devise was to increase his speed as if to cross the danger zone as quickly as possible. As it happened, this had the desired effect. The shadow moved swiftly, and at the same time altered its shape, thus revealing a change of position; and Biggles's expression hardened as he realised fully for the first time that had he not been aware of what was going on, or had the Sultan been flying the machine, he would have no hope of escape. What Rocky intended was plain, cold-blooded murder.

Well, Biggles was ready. It was no longer necessary to watch the shadow, for the other machine, having moved out of the sun, was now in plain view, perhaps a quarter of a mile to his left and slightly above him. He recognised the type, and knew that

Laroula was watching him from his cockpit. It was on the Cobra that Biggles now kept his eyes, his left foot resting lightly on the rudder-bar and his right hand firm on the control column.

Suddenly the nose of the Cobra tilted down; it swung round to cover him and he knew that the moment had come. His left foot kicked hard. The result was a wild skid that brought his nose round without appreciably altering his line of flight. His body was pressed by centrifugal force against the side of the cockpit; but the ultimate effect was to cause the tracer bullets intended for him to stream harmlessly past the tip of his port wing.

Biggles did not dally in his response. Once more he was a war pilot. The other man was his proven enemy in a deadly game that two could play, and he had no compunction about retaliating. Indeed, he went to work with zest, for there was a personal element about this that was absent from normal combat, when each man is fighting for his side. Cordova was just a crook, actuated solely by personal gain.

Biggles's nose went down, with the throttle wide open; and as he went down he turned. Straight under his opponent he went so fast that Laroula must have wondered what had become of him. He, too, turned slowly, presumably looking for him; but by that time Biggles was in the eye of the sun, already coming back. As the Cobra floated into his sights his guns spurted, and it was with grim satisfaction that he saw the burst go home. The Cobra appeared to stagger under the impact.

Never were tables more well and truly turned. Laroula, who had come prepared to slay a sheep, must have been shocked to discover that he had struck at a tiger. No doubt it was due to this that he made only an amateurish attempt to save himself, although, admittedly, Biggles did not give him time properly to recover. The Cobra was still weaving helplessly, with its pilot looking for his opponent, when Biggles struck again, from behind, and that, for all practical purposes, was the end. The Cobra went into a steep sideslip towards the ground, trailing petrol vapour as if its tanks had been holed; and had Laroula gone on down there is just a chance that he might have reached the ground alive. But he must have completely lost his head—or so Biggles afterwards opined. Recovering from the first shock, and actuated possibly by a desire to hit back, the Mexican suddenly pulled up his nose in a climbing turn and fired at where he supposed his enemy to be.

The result was instantly fatal. As the tracer swept through the vapour trail that he himself had made there was a vivid flash of flame—which, it may be said, gave Biggles a fright, for following the machine down he was uncomfortably close to it. He sheered off abruptly. By the time he was clear, and able to look down, the Cobra was cartwheeling in a mass of flames across the River of Gold that had in truth become a stream of death.

Biggles circled, but did not land. Knowing that no one in the machine could have survived, he saw no point in risking his life in a rescue effort that could only be futile. For a minute or two he remained, looking down with an expressionless face at the scattered wreckage that held the remains of the man whose hobby was collecting diamonds— other people's diamonds.

As he turned away, a shadow fell across his cockpit and he looked up sharply to see Ginger standing by. He raised a hand and pointed to the north.

Side by side the two Mosquitoes turned their tails to the scene of the tragedy and cruised on towards a more fertile land.

The same evening British newspapers reported that His Highness, the Sultan of Lashanti, and his son, had arrived in London for the Colonial Conference. Just that and nothing more. As far as Biggles was concerned it was enough.

THE CASE OF THE UNREGISTERED OPERATOR

THE door of the Air Police Operations Room at Gatwick Airport opened to admit a heavily built, bowler-hatted man, well known by sight to Biggles. It was Inspector Gaskin of "C" Department, C.I.D., New Scotland Yard.

"Hallo, Inspector! What crooked trail brings you here?" greeted Biggles cheerfully, pushing forward a chair.

The Inspector sat down and mopped a broad brow with a large handkerchief. "It's warm outside," he commented.

"Kind of," agreed Biggles. "You know my boys, I think," he added, indicating Ginger, Bertie and Algy, who were in the room.

"I've heard plenty about them, anyway," stated the Inspector.

"What's your trouble?" enquired Biggles, opening a box of cigarettes.

"I've just been talking to your Chief, Air Commodore Raymond, and as you weren't around he suggested that I ran down to have a word with you," explained the detective.

"If it's something you can't handle, it must be pretty sticky," observed Biggles.

"It isn't that we can't handle it, but—er—well——"

"You're finding the going heavy, eh?" suggested Biggles, smiling.

"That's about it," admitted the Inspector.

"Let's have the problem, and if it's in our line maybe we can suggest something," invited Biggles.

"That's just it. I have come to the conclusion that it *is* in your line," asserted the Inspector.

"Go ahead," requested Biggles.

The detective cleared his throat. "A week ago Charlie Cotelli, the cracksman, was discharged from prison after a five-year stretch. That was at eight in the morning. At eight the same evening he broke into Plevington Castle and lifted jewellery worth six thousand quid. We know he did it because he has his own way of working, which marks him as plain as if he plastered everything with finger prints."

"So now you're looking for Charlie?" suggested Biggles.

"No," answered the Inspector shortly. "That's just it. We're not. We know where he is. He's in Belfast. He was there the same night, throwing his weight about in a pub in a way that suggests he was making a point of being seen. You see, if he was in Belfast he couldn't have lifted Lady Plevington's sparklers. In other words, he's got a cast-iron alibi. Get the idea?"

Biggles nodded.

"How did he get there?" questioned the Inspector.

"I can answer that," returned Biggles. "He flew. He couldn't have got there any other way in the time."

"Exactly. All right. A month ago, just about dusk, Joe Lasker, the smash-and-grab specialist, pushed a spanner through the window of a Bond Street jeweller and got away with a tray of rings worth eight thousand pounds. He was seen by a constable on point duty who recognised him. We got busy looking for Joe, but we had to give up because it couldn't have been him. He was in Paris when the spanner went through the window. That's what he'll say, and we couldn't give him the lie, because somewhere about two hours later he was spotted by a French *agent* going into a low dive in Montparnasse. Another alibi. I could give you other cases of the same sort of thing, but that should be enough. If the game isn't stopped there'll be more, because if there's one thing that sticks out like a sore finger it's this: these get-aways are being organised by somebody with brains."

"Not only brains," murmured Biggles. "This smart guy also has an aircraft."

"That's what we reckon," said the Inspector gloomily. "How are we going to stop it?"

"Is that what you came down to ask me?"

"It is. You're the only man we've got who knows how to chase aeroplanes."

"As a matter of fact, Inspector, I suspect you've given me a line on something that's been worrying me, too," asserted Biggles. "For a couple of months or more I've been getting reports from the Air Ministry to the effect that their radar operators have been picking up an aircraft that they are unable to trace. First it was off the east coast; then the west; and on two occasions off the south coast. We haven't a clue as to who it is. True, I wasn't thinking of a machine giving the underworld the run-around. The pilot, whoever he is, is breaking every rule of the Air Navigation Code and is a menace to civil machines operating on regular routes. One day there'll be a collision, with big loss of life. Apart from which, if it comes to the knowledge of airline pilots that an unlicensed machine is tearing about the sky they'll get the jitters. There's nothing like the possibility of a collision to put a pilot's nerves on edge."

"Huh! Well, that hooks up, anyway," averred the Inspector. "Now I'll tell you something else. A little while ago there was a rumour going round the shadier sorts of London night clubs that if anyone wanted to go abroad without the usual formalities it could be arranged—for a consideration. That, too, sounds like aviation. We put a stool-pigeon on the job. He's been hanging around the night clubs for the past fortnight letting it be known that he was on the run; but so far no one has come to him with an offer of help."

Biggles shook his head. "I am afraid that may have been a bit too obvious. We're dealing with a wise guy."

"Well, what are we going to do about it?" queried the Inspector. "Can't you go up one night and catch this fellow red-handed?"

Biggles looked pained. "Have a heart, Inspector. How many planes do you suppose it would need to watch two thousand miles of coastline, bearing in mind that this mystery kite might be flying at anything from one to twenty thousand feet? No, that isn't the way to catch him. But just a minute. There's a point in your story that strikes me as odd, and it may give me a line to work on. You say Cotelli came out of gaol, did a job, and got out of the country the same night. How did *he* get in touch with this obliging pilot? He couldn't have heard about him while he was inside; and it seems extraordinary that he could do that, and crack a crib into the bargain, within a few hours of being released. Somebody must have put in some fast work."

The Inspector nodded. "Yes, that's true. The thing must have been all fixed up on the outside. Does that suggest anything to you?"

Biggles lit a cigarette with thoughtful deliberation.

"It's right up your street," prompted the detective.

"I'm not denying it," replied Biggles quietly. "Don't worry, I'll do something. Give me an hour or two to think the thing over. I don't know much about men with criminal records, so I may need your co-operation. However, we'll see."

The Inspector got up. "All right. We'll leave it like that then. I'll do anything I can. Now I must get back to the Yard. See you later. So long. So long, boys." He went out.

Biggles drew pensively on his cigarette for some minutes.

"Well, what do you make of it?" asked Algy presently.

"One thing, so far," answered Biggles. "Cotelli didn't find this bloke who keeps an aircraft in his back-yard. The bloke found him. If it worked that way once, it might happen again. It's the only line we have to work on, so I think I'll try it."

Two days later, for the first time in his life, Biggles sat in the cell of a British convict prison. Outside, London was just starting its day's work, for the time was 7.45 a.m. The grey suit he wore did not fit him very well, which was no matter for surprise, for it had been issued to him only half an hour earlier from the store from which prisoners going out drew garments, should they require them.

For the rest, the appointments of the cell did not conform to what might normally have been expected. There was a comfortable chair. Some magazines and newspapers lay on a table, with a breakfast-tray suitable for a first-class hotel.

Smoking a cigarette reflectively, Biggles reached for one of the newspapers, one bearing the date of the previous day, and a faint smile crossed his face as he looked, not for the first time, at a small paragraph on the front page. This is what he read:

"J. A. Bensil, the bank cashier who, it may be recalled, was sent to prison for absconding with nearly £10,000 in treasury notes, is due for release tomorrow morning, having served his full sentence rather than divulge what he did with the money, which, in consequence, has never been recovered."

Above this item of news was a rather blurred photograph of himself without collar or tie. The caption read, J. A. Bensil.

The door opened and Inspector Gaskin entered. Seeing what Biggles was looking at, he enquired: "Is that what you wanted?"

"Just the thing," answered Biggles.

"Sure there's nothing else I can do?"

"Not a thing."

"You're playing a dangerous game, you know."

"It won't be the first time," murmured Biggles.

"Even so, you keep out of the way. Just stick to the

programme. The man I'm hoping to meet will be smart enough to know that he's being followed, should anyone try it. The only weak part of our scheme is, it would be natural if the police did follow me. They must still be hoping to find the £10,000 I pinched, and I'm the only man who can lead them to it. However, we'll leave things as they are."

The detective shrugged. "Okay. You know what you're doing—I hope. If you're ready, the Governor is waiting for you."

The prison Governor was, in fact, at the door. "Come on, Bensil!" he said; but there was a twinkle in his eye, for he was of necessity a party to the scheme.

Leaving the detective in the cell, Governor and prisoner walked briskly to the main gate, Biggles carrying a mackintosh on his arm. The grim portal was opened by the warder on duty. The Governor held out a hand. "I hope, after this, you'll go straight," he said loudly, the corners of his mouth twitching.

"One night in that gloomy barrack of yours should be enough to last anyone for the rest of his days," said Biggles softly.

"I wish they all thought that," replied the Governor sadly. "Well, good luck."

"Thank you, sir." Biggles turned away, and looking neither to left nor right, without a glance behind him, strode down the pavement.

Not until he was in Lambeth Street was there any indication that his plan might produce results. Then, suddenly, a dark saloon car, with a rear window wound down, glided in beside the kerb. "Want a lift?" said a voice.

Biggles turned his head and saw two men in the car. One, the driver, a small, well-dressed man, was looking ahead. The other, sitting behind, a big, fresh-complexioned type, was looking at him, smiling. "No thanks," answered Biggles, and walked on.

The car moved with him. "Can't we take you anywhere—Bensil?" said the man in the rear seat.

Biggles turned his head again sharply at this use of his assumed name. "What's the idea?" he demanded curtly.

"Thought you might do with a lift."

"No thanks, I can manage," returned Biggles, tight-lipped.

"You haven't got a hope," said the man in the car. "The cops are watching you. They'll never take their eyes off you while you've got that dough."

The corners of Biggles's mouth came down. "Is that so? What's it to you, anyway?"

"We could help."

"Who are you?"

The man grinned. "Call us the P.P.A.—the Personal Protection Association."

Biggles glanced quickly up and down the road before he answered. "And how do you reckon you can help?"

"You'll see. Get in." The door swung open invitingly.

Biggles hesitated for a moment like a man unable to make up his mind. "Okay. I'll try it," he said, and ducked swiftly into the car.

He was literally flung into his seat as the driver accelerated. Accustomed as he was to travelling at high speeds, he held his breath as the car dodged in and out of the traffic. "Here! Take it easy," he complained.

"We're only losing anyone who happened to be interested in where you were going," said his companion. "Don't worry. Slick's a good driver. He's used to moving fast."

Biggles said no more. He soon lost all idea of where he was, for Slick turned and turned again in a maze of narrow streets for a good ten minutes before making a lightning swerve through a narrow entrance into a yard. Even then the car did not stop, but shot straight into a garage, the doors of which were slammed by unseen hands.

They got out. Slick opened a door in the wall. "This way," he said casually.

A short corridor, a flight of stairs, and Biggles found himself in a small room with one window which overlooked a street. In the brief interval of time allowed him he saw two landmarks. One was a neon sign advertising a brand of whisky, on the wall of the house opposite; the other was the top of an 11E bus. By this time a door had been opened and he was ushered into a well-furnished apartment of some size. A dark, smartly dressed man, with an unusually high forehead, was doing something with some glasses and bottles at a sideboard. Looking over his shoulder at Biggles, he said: "Have a drink! You must need one. Give it a name."

"I never touch alcohol, it doesn't agree with me—thanks all the same," declined Biggles.

"Just as you like. Sit down." The man, and the two who had been in the car, helped themselves to drinks. With a glass in his hand, the dark man, whom Biggles had already decided was the leader of the party, dropped into an easy chair opposite the one Biggles had taken. "Here's luck," said he, taking a drink. "Cigarette?"

"Thanks." This time Biggles accepted the offer.

"And now," went on the dark man, "suppose we skip the preamble and get down to business. Where are you going? What are you going to do, and how do you reckon you're going to get away with the money you hid, without the police being there to snatch it off you?"

"That's my affair," answered Biggles slowly. "I've had plenty of time to think about it," he added grimly.

There were smiles at this pointed remark.

"Now look here, Bensil, let me give you a bit of advice," resumed the dark man seriously. "Keep away from that money or you'll lose it. I had you picked up to help you to get it. Naturally I hope to get some for myself at the same time. I don't deny that. But I am willing to do something for my share."

"And just what do you think you can do?" asked Biggles.

"You're finished as far as this country's concerned," declared the dark man. "Your lay is to go abroad, taking the dough with you. That's where I come in. I can take you where you like, with the money, without snoopers wanting to know what's in your bag. That's something you couldn't manage yourself."

"And what do you want for this—er—service?"

"Twenty per cent."

Biggles frowned. "£2,000! That's too much. It represents twelve months of the time I've done. You want it for one day's work."

"I don't get it all for myself," was the sharp reply. "It has to be cut several ways, and expenses are high."

"You wouldn't do so badly if you took a thousand," asserted Biggles. "That's as far as I'm prepared to go."

The dark man glanced at his companions. "Let's split the difference," he suggested. "Call it £1,500."

"Split it again and call it £1,250. That's my limit," said Biggles in a voice as if he meant it.

"Okay—twelve fifty. Now, where's the dough?"

"What do you want to know for?"

"So we can fetch it. It wouldn't be safe for you to go near it."

Biggles smiled a smile that was faintly derisive. "What do you take me for? I'm nothing to you. If I tell you where it is there's nothing to stop you taking the lot and leaving me to whistle."

"Quite right, only we don't work that way."

"I've only your word for it, and as I don't know you that isn't enough."

"You can come with us. At the moment the police don't know where you are. But they'll be looking, make no mistake about that, and you won't get far on your own without one of their plain-clothes men spotting you."

"Suppose I come with you," replied Biggles. "What's to prevent you, when you get your hands on the stuff, knocking me on the head and throwing me into the nearest river?"

"Nothing," answered the dark man, with surprising frankness. "You'll have to trust us."

"What about you trusting me?"

"How?"

"I'll collect the stuff and send you your share through the post."

The other shook his head. "I've told you, you couldn't get it without being picked up."

"I could—if I was in the country where I hid it. The police there don't know me."

"And where's that?"

"France."

The dark man whistled softly and glanced at his accomplices. "That's something I didn't bargain for." He looked back at Biggles. "How did you get it there?"

"Posted it in the ordinary way, in case the police picked me up before I could get over there myself. Knowing what I was going to do, I had an address ready to post it to—a little flat in Paris owned by a relation of mine. So before we can carve up the stuff, we've got to get to it. How are you going to manage that?"

"Easy. I'll fly you over. That happens to be my line of business."

"All right," agreed Biggles slowly. "You fly me over. We'll go to the flat. I'll give you your cut, after which we can go our own ways. I shall stay in Paris."

"Fair enough," agreed the dark man.

"When do we go?"

"Tonight. The sooner the better. Obviously we don't work in daylight."

"That's okay with me," confirmed Biggles.

"Meanwhile, you'd better stay here out of harm's

way. We'll make you comfortable," promised the dark man. "Incidentally, if you want to change your sterling into francs I'll tell you the name of a man who'll give you the best rates and no questions asked."

"He's in the black market, eh?"

"In it?" The man laughed scornfully. "He's the king of it. Now you can take it easy while we get things fixed up. Just one last point." The man's dark eyes found Biggles's. His hand went to his pocket to reveal the butt of an automatic. "No funny stuff—or else."

Biggles smiled. "That's a good argument, anyhow," he murmured, helping himself to another cigarette.

At eight o'clock the same evening the dark man —whom Biggles had heard referred to by his assistants, appropriately, as Darkie—came in and announced that it was time to move off. The others were not there, and Biggles wondered if they were to be left behind, but when they got to the car, using the same route by which they had gained admission to the house, the driver of the morning was in his place. The fresh-complexioned man did not put in an appearance.

The car set off. Where it was going Biggles had no idea. All he knew was that his destination was about an hour's run from London. The night, he saw, not without misgivings—for like most pilots he

detested being flown by anyone he did not know—
was dark and overcast. The car left London on the
Great West Road; but he learned no more than that,
for shortly afterwards his companion drew the
blinds and he could think of no reasonable excuse
for demanding that they should be lifted.

It was about an hour later that the car made a
sharp turn and at the same time slowed down on a
piece of road so rough that it was obviously a lane
or farm track. Within five minutes the end came
suddenly. The car stopped. "This is it," said
Darkie. "Come on." He got out.

Biggles followed, and found that the car had
halted in a stubble field of some size. Close at hand,
near a clump of elms, was a double line of corn-
stacks. The car did not wait. With its head-lights
dimmed, turning in the field, it went slowly down
the lane that gave access to it.

Darkie walked briskly to the corn-stacks. Biggles
went with him, and there, under a tarpaulin
stretched between them and covered with straw,
stood an aircraft—a Puss Moth of ancient vintage.
There was nobody with it. The only light shone
from the window of a cottage or farmhouse about
two hundred yards away. But a minute later twin
beams of headlights cut a flare path across the field,
and Biggles smiled in the darkness as he realised that
the car had simply moved to a position from which
it could act as a beacon.

c

Darkie opened the door of the aircraft. "Get in," he ordered.

They got in. The door slammed. The starter whirred. The engine sprang to life. A minute passed, with the engine idling. Then it roared, and the aircraft raced across the field. Darkie was staring into the darkness ahead; and so, for that matter, was Biggles, who was by no means happy. However, the wheels were soon off the ground. The machine swept up and round in an unnecessarily steep climbing turn, and then, still climbing, settled down on a southerly course.

Looking down, Biggles saw what he had under-taken the flight to ascertain—the location of the secret airfield. The Great West Road, with its streams of traffic lights and an illuminated sign on the factory of a firm of publishers, told him the position of it exactly.

"Ever been up before?" asked Darkie.

"Once or twice," murmured Biggles blandly.

"You ought to learn to fly yourself, you never know when it may come in handy," advised Darkie.

"I shall have to think about it," returned Biggles in a steady voice. "Have you been flying long?" he enquired.

"Seven years. I used to be a night-flying instructor." The man laughed bitterly. "They threw me out because I brought a few things home from France—and forgot to declare them. True,

I made money out of it—but who wouldn't, given the chance? A few bob a day service pay was no use to me."

"And you think you can get away with this?"

"What's to stop me? Pah! It's money for old rope. I've got the mechanic who used to unload the stuff I brought from France giving me a hand."

Biggles said no more. There was no need. He knew, now, all he wanted to know.

In half an hour they were over the Channel, Darkie having cut his engine to glide over the coast. Ten minutes later this manoeuvre was repeated as he crossed the coast of France. Rather more than an hour later the machine touched down at a spot which Biggles judged to be not more than a twenty minutes' run by car from Paris.

The machine ran to a standstill near some farm buildings. "I'll leave her here," said Darkie. "I shall be back again presently. Don't worry about the farmer—he's all right. One of the gang, in fact."

"How do we get to Paris?"

"Car. I keep one here. Simple, isn't it?" Darkie laughed again, presumably at his own cleverness. As they got into the car he asked: "What's the address?"

"Forty-one rue Chantonesse. It's by the river near the Ile de Paris. I'll show you."

The short drive passed without incident, and under Biggles's direction the car pulled up against the kerb in a quiet, dimly-lighted street. Biggles went to the door and knocked. The *concierge*, an elderly man, answered, and stood aside to allow the two callers to enter. Biggles led the way to the first floor, entered a room the door of which stood ajar, and switched on the electric light. "Here we are," he said cheerfully, and going over to a cupboard took out a suitcase which he put on a table. He was about to open it when he started, staring at something Darkie held in his hand. It was the automatic.

"What's the idea?" he asked sharply.

"The idea is I'll take care of that suitcase," replied Darkie crisply.

"But you—what about——?"

"Okay, brother. Take it easy. Keep your mouth shut and you won't get hurt. Start squealing and you will," snapped Darkie viciously.

"I think you're just the lowest type of crook," said Biggles coldly.

"What you think won't lose *me* any sleep," said Darkie, grinning unpleasantly.

Biggles regarded him with contempt. "You never made a bigger mistake in your life. There was a moment when I could have felt sorry for you. How wrong I should have been. You're just a cheap crook after all." Then, raising his voice, he went on: "Okay, Inspector, help yourself."

There must have been something in Biggles's

manner that told Darkie the truth, for he spun round. Biggles jumped in, grabbed the hand that held the gun, and bent it back over his own arm. At the same moment into the room hurried Inspector Gaskin with another plain-clothes man and two uniformed gendarmes.

The struggle was short. The automatic went off, but all the bullet did was tear a hole in the carpet. Upon this, the Inspector's heavy fist flew out. It took Darkie on the point of the jaw and sent him sprawling.

"Try that game on me, would you?" growled the Inspector wrathfully, as he kicked the pistol aside and picked it up. Then he looked at Biggles and smiled.

"Nice work, Inspector," complimented Biggles quietly. "You got things organised over this side very nicely."

The Inspector indicated his plain-clothes companion. "Meet Captain Joudrier of the *Sûreté.*"

Biggles nodded. "Glad to know you, Captain. Thanks for your co-operation." He turned to Darkie, now in the grip of the gendarmes. "I forgot to mention that Inspector Gaskin flew over this afternoon with a suitcase stuffed with old newspapers to find a nice quiet apartment for our reception. Now I'm going back to make arrangements for your reception on the other side of the Channel." To the Inspector he went on: "I'll tell you where you can find the machine that brought us over. It had better stay where it is, for evidence, until our French colleagues have picked up the farmer. He's in the gang. They'll also be interested to know the name of the king of the black market over here. I can give it to them. I'm not much for flying strange machines, so I'll ring my boys and get one of them over to fetch me. When you get back I'll give you the gen on the rest of this bunch. I know where they can be found."

"Good enough," agreed Inspector Gaskin. "As I said earlier on, you boys certainly do work fast."

"That's what aeroplanes are for," Biggles reminded him as he turned toward the stairs.

THE CASE OF THE WOUNDED AGENT

Biggles signed his weekly report, closed his office desk, put the keys in his pocket and got up.

"That's enough for today," he told his waiting staff. "As things are now all quiet on the skyway, you lazy cloud-cops can trickle off and continue misspending your miserable lives. I'm going round to the Aero Club for a quiet evening with the foreign aviation magazines." He reached for his hat.

At that moment the inter-com telephone buzzed sharply.

He picked up the receiver, and his eyes glanced meaningly round those watching him as he listened. "Right away, sir," he said, and replaced the instrument.

"Seems I spoke out of turn," he remarked quietly. "Keep your hands off the throttle till I come back. I may need you. Judging from the Chief's tone of voice there's something not only cooking, but scorching." He went out.

Two minutes later he walked into the office of Air Commodore Raymond, Assistant Commissioner of Police. He found him standing with his back to an empty fireplace, hands thrust deep into his pockets.

"Come in, Bigglesworth," invited the Air Commodore. "I won't ask you to sit down—there isn't time."

Biggles waited.

The Air Commodore drew a deep breath. "Now listen carefully," he said. "You belong to this department. You've plenty to do, and I dislike the idea of lending you to anyone else. But I'm on a spot. The trouble is, you're getting too well known, and unless I keep you locked in your own hangar you're liable to find yourself a sort of dog's-body for every Tom, Dick and Harry from one end of Whitehall to the other."

Biggles smiled.

"Five minutes ago a very important person concerned with national security rang me up to know if I could recommend a pilot for an extremely urgent job calling for nerve, resource and discretion. What could I say? I couldn't say 'no', because, in the first place, it would have been a lie, and, secondly, it would have implied that I had nothing on my staff but nitwits. I told him that I had just such a pilot as he needed—which he already knew perfectly well. I also had to admit that we had machines available for any class of operation."

"Assuming that you're talking about me, I can feel my face going red," murmured Biggles. "Thank you. What is it that this very important person wants?"

"I don't know. I didn't ask. He wouldn't have discussed the matter over the telephone, anyway. You'd better go and ask him—that is, if you feel inclined to volunteer for the job. You can please yourself about that. It's outside my department, so you'd be quite in order in declining. Once I start lending you someone will always be in need of a pilot." The Air Commodore spoke bitterly.

Biggles took a cigarette from his case and tapped it thoughtfully on the back of his hand. "This chap must be hard pushed for a pilot of particular experience or he wouldn't have come to you," he observed. "What's wrong with the Air Force? They've plenty of good pilots."

"That's what I told them, but he said he daren't use a serving officer."

Biggles lit his cigarette and flicked the dead match into the fireplace. "That gives us an idea of the sort of job it is," he said softly. "If it's a matter of national emergency we can't let him down. I'd better go and see what he wants."

"I'll take you round."

"Mind if I use your phone?"

"Go ahead."

Biggles picked up the inter-com. Ginger's voice answered. Biggles spoke briefly. "I'm going out for a few minutes. Stand fast till I come back." He hung up and followed his Chief into the yard, where a car was waiting.

They hadn't far to go. In less than ten minutes they were being shown by a uniformed messenger into a typical Whitehall office where, waiting to receive them, stood an elderly, tired-faced man, who, nevertheless, had about him an air of quiet efficiency.

The Air Commodore made the introductions. "Charles, this is Bigglesworth, the pilot we were speaking about. Bigglesworth, this is Major Charles, of the counter-espionage section of M.I.5."

The Intelligence officer nodded unsmilingly. "Sit down," he requested, and then turned penetrating eyes on Biggles. "So you're Bigglesworth. I've heard of you, of course. You've been around a bit, I believe."

"I've seen as much of the world as most people," admitted Biggles.

"How well do you know the Balkans?"

"Not very well."

"Macedonia—Northern Greece?"

Biggles shook his head. "I may have flown over, but not with any particular interest, so I can't say I know it."

"No matter. You can find your way there?"

"Certainly."

"Very well. The area in which I'm interested is at the western end of the frontier with Bulgaria. As you may know, there has been a lot of trouble there lately—Greek revolutionaries, communists, bandits, guerillas of all sorts, and heaven knows what, all fighting each other to oblige one or two political grafters who would like to own the country. With them I'm not particularly concerned. I'm interested in one man only. His real name and nationality are of no importance. He's a British agent, and one of the best men I have in that part of the world. He will answer to the name of Maxos. He speaks English. Where he has been is of no concern to you, but he has in his possession, gained at fearful risks, a certain document which I am very anxious to have. He was making his way to Greece, where we have friends, with every hostile agent looking for him, when, by sheer bad luck, he was struck in the thigh by a bullet, fired either by one of his pursuers or by a casual rebel—we don't know which. He managed to crawl into cover, and there he is at this moment. He may be alive or he may be dead. I have lost touch with him. One thing's certain; he's no longer able to travel. I want the papers he has on his person. I haven't another man near enough to reach him on foot in time to do any good. Flying is the only hope. You follow?"

Biggles nodded.

"The man's position is roughly on a line between Demphos and Petritza. These are villages about seven miles apart. You'll find them on the map. The terrain, as far as I'm able to describe it, is what is usually called rolling country. In places it is flat and fertile, but there are rough areas with timber-covered hills. Until a few hours ago Maxos was in touch with me by walkie-talkie radio and able to tell me what had happened. His signals were getting weak and soon afterwards faded out. There's no need for me to tell you what I want you to do. All I want to know is, will you do it?"

"Of course," answered Biggles without hesitation.

"Very well. You know better than I do what will be necessary so make your own arrangements. Speed is everything. I'm sorry I can't tell you more about the nature of the country at that particular spot. There may be no flat patch large enough for you to land upon. If that turns out to be the case, how you'll get down—or having got down, how you'll get off again—I don't know. That's your business. If it comes to a crash landing, don't worry about the aircraft. Burn it, and get home any way you can. Take plenty of money. I'll send you over a supply of currency likely to be useful in emergency. Save the man if you can, but, alive or dead, get the papers. If he's still alive no doubt he'll show himself to you because he knows that I'm trying to get a rescue plane to him. If he's dead, or unconscious—well, the job of finding him may be rather more difficult."

Biggles smiled at this flagrant under-statement. To find a man who had hidden himself from observation, in such wild country, was likely to be more than difficult, he thought.

"One or two final points," went on Major Charles. "Your aircraft must carry no nationality marks, military or civil, or someone will start a scream about flying over foreign territory without official sanction. There's no time for that. In any case, you know what happens to any aircraft flying behind the Iron Curtain. You will certainly be shot at if you're seen; and if you're shot down, that'll be the last we shall hear of you. But I needn't enlarge on the risks of the undertaking. With your experience they must be apparent to you."

"I'll see what I can do about it," promised Biggles.

"Any more questions?"

"None. You want me to fetch the papers—and the man if he's still alive."

"Exactly."

"Then as he is wounded, the sooner I'm on my way the better."

"I think so. There's no particular urgency about the papers once you have them in your possession. As long as you get them to me I shall be satisfied. When will you start?"

"Tonight. I shall be over the objective by dawn."

"Good." Major Charles got up and held out a hand. "Best of luck!"

"Thanks." Biggles shook hands, and without speaking returned with the Air Commodore to the Yard.

"Anything you want from me?" asked the Air

Commodore as they parted. "Anything I can do . . . ?"

"There's just one thing," answered Biggles thoughtfully. "I shall take the long-range Auster for the job, but I shall have to refuel somewhere. Brindisi would do. Speaking from memory that's about two hundred and fifty miles from the objective. You might smooth things out for me there—Customs, petrol, and so on—through the International Police Commission."

"I'll do that."

"I shall tell the others about this business," went on Biggles. "Then, if I don't get back they can have a shot at it. One of us should pull it off. In fact, Ginger can follow me out and wait at Brindisi. He'll be handy to have a crack at it if I fail, and he'll be on the spot to give me a hand, should I need it, if I get through. I'm thinking of the man Maxos. I'll save him if it's possible; but if he's badly hurt he'll need medical attention. You might have an ambulance standing by at Brindisi, in case. Is that all right with you?"

"As long as you get those papers anything will be all right with me," asserted the Air Commodore. "It's your show. Manage it your own way. Be careful."

"I always am," murmured Biggles as he walked on.

Twelve hours later, from five thousand feet, Biggles watched the dawn break, chill and cheerless, through the whirling arc of the airscrew as his Auster drove an eastward course over what appeared to be a lifeless land of rolling plains and rocky hills. Of the fertile areas of which Major Charles had spoken little could be seen, either on account of early-morning mist that hung in the valleys or because the peasants who should have tilled the soil had abandoned homes stricken by the curse of civil war. Only the irregular patches of timber stood out darkly against a background that was for the most part colourless.

Biggles's eyes moved ceaselessly, from earth to sky, and occasionally to his instrument panel, which told him that he was nearing his objective. That eyes on the ground were watching him he did not doubt, for an aircraft cannot move in daylight without being seen; but it was from eyes in the sky, that would, he knew, appear when his presence was reported, that he had most to fear. There was a certain amount of cloud about, and behind the curtain it provided he had remained for most of his passage across Eastern Europe; but now, in order to see what lay below, he had been forced into the open. Dead reckoning had taken him to the vital area, but he could not rely on long range navigation to reveal the villages between which lay the man he had come so far to find.

From the height at which he flew he hoped to pick out both villages and take a course between them;

and this in fact he did; at least, with no conspicuous landmarks to guide him he had to assume that they were the hamlets he sought. One appeared to be in ruins. From the other smoke drifted sluggishly into the air, either from kitchens or smouldering homes; he could not be sure which. Not that it mattered overmuch as he was not concerned with the actual villages. His hand moved to the throttle. The nose of the aircraft tilted down as the engine died. The Auster glided on, losing height slowly, the air whispering softly over the plane surfaces.

Looking over his shoulder Biggles studied the sky behind him with the calculating efficiency of long practice, seeking a moving speck which he feared might be there. But there was nothing, nothing except wisps of fleecy alto-cirrus cloud aglow with the reflected light of the rising sun. Satisfied that, for the moment at any rate, he was not being shadowed, he returned his attention to the ground.

It was much as he expected to find it, but, even so, regarded in cold blood he was dismayed by the seemingly hopeless task that he had set himself. Right across the landscape, cutting at right-angles across the area under survey, ran two ravines, their sides buried under a blanket of vegetation. Between these stood a pinewood of some size. For the rest, the ground appeared to be mostly barren, stony earth, for the greater part uneven, with occasional groups of ancient olive trees, conspicuous by their silvery foliage.

It was quite evident to Biggles that if the man he sought had died in his hiding-place a score of men might search for him for weeks in vain. But the big question that exercised his mind was whether to remain in the air or try to get down. There were arguments for and against both possibilities. If the man was still alive he would hear the aircraft, in which case it might reasonably be supposed that he would reveal himself. If he did, he would be more easily spotted from the air than from ground level. On the other hand, if he, Biggles, landed, he might choose a spot miles from the wounded man. Not that there was much choice in the matter of a landing ground. The Auster was slow, and could get down in an area much smaller than would be required for a fast machine; which was, of course, why he had employed that particular type. Naturally he was anxious to get down as close as possible to his man, for he realised that by this time he must have been seen by hostile eyes and his presence reported. At the most he could not reckon on more than an hour free from molestation.

In the end he decided to compromise. He would first fly low over the important area to make sure that Maxos, if he were still alive, would see him and expose himself. If this failed, he would land on such places as were available in the hope that Maxos would have enough strength to reach him. As a plan it was far from satisfactory, but there was nothing more he could do.

Putting it into action, he swung low over the first village and took up a course for the second. Looking down as he passed over the primitive dwellings he saw groups of men standing in the street staring up at him. Others were hurrying out to join them. Significantly, there were no women. Then he observed that some of the men carried rifles, and that told him all he needed to know. The village was occupied by a military force, but whether by Government troops, rebels or bandits it was impossible to tell.

He flew on, banking in alternate directions, blipping his engine—the only signal he could make to announce his arrival—eyes scanning the ground, first on one side of the machine then the other, looking both for Maxos and possible landing-places. In this way he covered half the distance without seeing a living soul. Once a bullet struck his machine, but of the man who had fired it he saw no sign. Never did a task seem more futile, and as he carried on it was more in hope than confidence of the outcome. He circled the pinewood. Nothing happened.

Straightening the Auster, he noticed a moving object on some open ground a fair distance from his line of flight. At first he took it to be an animal grazing; indeed, had any such animals been in evidence it is unlikely that he would have given it a second glance; but it struck him suddenly as odd that of the many domestic animals that must at one time have occupied the ground one only should have survived. Swinging round, he headed towards it, easing the control column forward for a closer look. Then he saw the object raise itself up, and recognised it for a man who had been crawling, but was now on his knees, an arm upraised.

Was it the man he had come to find, or was it some wretched fellow who had been wounded and abandoned in recent fighting? He didn't know, and as the only way of finding out was by landing he looked about quickly for a suitable place. One thing was at once apparent. There was nowhere near at hand. The terrain all around was rough, stony ground, uneven and dotted about with sprawling olive trees.

A swift search of the whole area revealed only one possible place, and even that could only be contemplated in the most desperate circumstances—as, of course, these were. It was a fairly level stretch of wild-looking country on the fringe of the pinewood. It was plenty large enough, but what worried him was the surface, which he could not see, as it was concealed under a yellowish growth of what he took to be long, sun-dried grass, weeds and small bushes. It was, comparatively speaking, some distance from the crawling man—a matter of not less than a quarter of a mile, which was further than he cared to leave his machine in order to get to him. But there was nowhere else, so with it he had to be content. There was a little wind, but fortunately it was in the right direction for the landing strip: so he side-slipped as the quickest way of losing height, flattened out and glided in alongside the wood and about thirty yards from it. There were several anxious seconds as the little aircraft bounced on small, hidden obstructions, and dragged through the long dry grass; but in the end it settled down on even keel. Biggles drew a swift breath of relief, switched off and jumped down.

After a penetrating stare around he ran on a little way ahead of the aircraft to make sure that there were no obstructions should he find it necessary to take off in a hurry. Satisfied that there were none, he turned about and ran for the place where he had seen the crawling man. On reaching him he found that he had made a little progress, but not very much. The man's face was pale and drawn with suffering and fatigue, and it was at once clear that he was near the end of his physical resources.

Biggles did not waste words. His business was too urgent. "Is your name Maxos?" he asked tersely.

"Yes," came the answer through bloodless lips.

"Your official number?"

"Ninety-one. Quick! Here are the papers. Take them and go. Never mind me."

Biggles took the packet and thrust it in his breast pocket. "You're coming with me," he announced. "No, no. It isn't possible. They're after me."

Biggles took a small brandy flask that he had brought for the purpose and made the man drink a little. "Don't argue," he said shortly. Then he helped him to his feet, got one arm round his shoulders, and started off for the machine.

Progress was slow, but steady, Maxos obviously making a supreme effort to keep going. But his strength gave out as they reached the nearest point of the wood, and he sank down. While he gave him a moment to rest Biggles ran on a little way, along the fringe of the wood, to make sure that all was well with the Auster. He soon saw that it was not. A dozen rough-looking, grey-uniformed men, armed with rifles, were galloping towards it from the opposite direction, apparently from a distance, having seen the machine land. There was, he thought, just time for him to reach the aircraft before they got to it; but the idea of leaving the wounded man to his fate was so repugnant that he did not even consider it.

He dived into the trees and hurried back to Maxos. "One more effort," he said encouragingly, and again they set off, keeping inside the wood. Under the sombre pines it was still only half light, which suited him well enough; and as the undergrowth consisted only of ferns they made fair progress.

It was just before they were level with the aircraft, and perhaps twenty yards inside the wood, that Maxos became aware of what had happened. The information came not from Biggles, but from the horsemen themselves, who were talking noisily—one, by the sound of it, giving orders. Maxos looked at Biggles. "Did you know?"

"Yes."

"You should have saved yourself," said Maxos sadly.

"When we start saving ourselves at the expense of friends we shan't have any friends," replied Biggles softly. "Don't worry. We'll manage somehow." He got his companion a little nearer to the machine, and then, leaving him lying under some ferns, crept forward to see what was happening.

The position was much as he expected to see it—perhaps somewhat better. At all events, the situation, he perceived, could have been worse had the men been disciplined troops under the command of a man who knew his job. Half of them were riding away, fan-wise, obviously looking for him. Of the six that remained, five had dismounted and had handed their mounts to the other, who, with his rifle slung and his arms through the reins, was lighting a cigarette. The five dismounted men were also smoking as they talked. But what brought a faint smile of derision to Biggles's face was the lazy way they had stacked their rifles against the fuselage of the aircraft. They may have thought they would not need them; or if they did, in such a position they would be handy. Upon such small things can big events depend.

For a moment Biggles surveyed the scene, his brain working fast, knowing that the longer the delay the more difficult would things become. Should more troops arrive the position would indeed be hopeless. Backing again to the wood, he returned to Maxos and told him to work his way forward as near to the edge of the wood as was possible without risk of being seen. Then, keeping in the deepest shadows, crouching low and picking his way carefully, he hastened to a point on the edge of the wood about a hundred yards above the aircraft, which, as he had of course landed into the wind, was up-wind from it. From his pocket he took a box of matches, lit one, and tossed it into the dry grass. Little yellow flames licked hungrily, and as a slant of wind caught them, raced forward, leaping and spreading, in the direction of the aircraft.

Biggles did not stop to watch their progress, but hurried back the way he had come, content that, if his plan failed, he would at least have destroyed the machine in accordance with his instructions. He hoped, of course, it would not come to that.

A yell of alarm told him that the fire had been seen, and, moving nearer to the edge of the wood, he saw the enemy behaving as he thought they would

—which was natural enough but not very sensible. With one accord they were running to the fire with the apparent intention of trying to put it out, forgetting in their haste to collect their weapons. Or they may have thought the rifles were safe where they were; perhaps they did not want to be encumbered with them. Anyhow, as Biggles had hoped, they left them leaning against the machine. Only one man remained by the Auster. His rifle was slung, and he was having difficulty with his charges, which were already restless as to their nostrils drifted the smoke of the fire.

Biggles raced back to Maxos, to find him, as he had ordered, on the edge of the wood. He gave him another nip of brandy, for the man was obviously done, and got him to his knees. "One more effort," he urged. "Try! Try hard! Now!" The man was too heavy for him to carry, so getting an arm under him he hauled him to his feet, and half led, half dragged him towards the machine. In his free hand he held his automatic. His eyes were on the man holding the horses, which were now on the point of stampeding and occupying all his attention.

Nevertheless, at the last moment the man saw him and let out a bellow of warning to his comrades.

Seeing that there was no longer any point in attempted concealment, Biggles fired a shot over the man's head. It only needed this to make the horses panic. They reared and bolted. The man, with his arm through the reins, was dragged from the saddle and fell heavily under the flying hooves. Biggles opened the door of the Auster and somehow managed to bundle Maxos inside. Slamming the door he ran to the other side, and, ignoring the rifles stacked against the fuselage, fired three shots at their owners, who by now had abandoned the fire and were tearing back towards the machine. They flung themselves flat as the bullets whistled past them. Another second and Biggles was in his seat, hand feeling for the starter. As the engine came to life the men got to their feet again and came on, but being unarmed, there was nothing they could do to stop the machine, which, with throttle wide open, came charging at them. Indeed, those who were in a direct line had to throw themselves flat again or swerve aside to avoid being knocked down.

One shot struck the machine somewhere. Where it came from Biggles never knew. His eyes were fixed ahead, on a wall of smoke that arose from a base of orange flames. The machine became airborne at the precise moment that it plunged into the smoke. For five seconds Biggles held his breath. Then he was through, in clean air, climbing for height, with the smoke between him and his enemies.

The danger passed, with a peculiar smile he looked at the man he had snatched from death.

But there was no answering smile. Maxos had slumped in his seat. His eyes were closed.

Biggles set a course for the west.

Rather less than two hours later he landed on the airfield near Brindisi. Ginger and a man he did not know came running out to meet him. Biggles jumped down and spoke quickly to Ginger. "You've got a machine here?"

"Yes."

"Tanks topped up?"

"All ready."

"Okay. Get those to Raymond. I'll see you later." Biggles handed over the packet of papers.

Ginger put them in his pocket and hurried away without another word.

Biggles spoke to the man who had remained. "Who are you?"

"I am Dr. Spanelli," was the answer. "I have a message from friends in London. You have perhaps a man who is hurt? Here I have an ambulance to take him to hospital."

Biggles indicated the unconscious Maxos. "Here's your patient, doctor," he said quietly. "I'll call to see him later. But first I must put my machine away and get a bite of breakfast. Can you manage?"

"Leave him to me."

"Thank you, doctor." Whistling softly, Biggles walked on towards the control office to check in.

THE CASE OF THE BRILLIANT PUPIL

"No doubt a lot of crooks have already realised the possibilities of aviation as a quick means of getting about; it'll be when they start flying themselves that we shall be kept busy." Detective Air-Inspector Bigglesworth, of the Special Air Police, smiled whimsically as he made the remark to Inspector Gaskin, of "C" Division, New Scotland Yard.

"That's just it," returned the Inspector gloomily. "I reckon they've started. That's what brings me down here today. It was your Chief who suggested to mine that I ran down and had a word with you about it—as if I hadn't enough to do, with that banknote robbery last week on my hands."

"Let's stick to aviation," suggested Biggles. "What's happened to give you the notion that crooks have started going to work in aeroplanes?"

"Not much—so far; but I've got an uneasy feeling that something will happen, and before very long."

"Tell me, what gave rise to this uneasy feeling?" requested Biggles. "Was it just a hunch?"

"I don't pay much regard to hunches," asserted the Inspector. "Facts are what I like." He took out a well-worn briar and thumbed tobacco into it pensively. "Ever hear of Toff Gestner?"

"No," admitted Biggles frankly. "Until I took on this job I managed to earn my daily crust without coming in contact with the ropey types who keep you guessing. Who's Toff Gestner?"

"Hubert Roland were the names given to him at his baptism. Toff was an appellation he picked up later, for reasons which you'll understand if ever you see him. He's one of these well-dressed, good-looking, oily-tongued fellows who seem to go crooked from choice. His people were well-off. They're dead now—died of heart-break, I reckon. Little Hubert was an only child and they gave him everything he wanted, which was probably too much. They sent him to a good school and he repaid them by getting himself expelled for petty theft. That was the start of a crooked trail that hasn't ended yet. He ran away from home, got mixed up with a tough gang, and so graduated for Borstal. By the time he was thirty he had served three prison sentences. At thirty-one he was sent down for three years' stretch for forgery. He came out twelve months ago and went off to Canada saying he was going to start a new life there. That's his record up to date." The Inspector lit his pipe which had gone out.

"Just when and how he got back to this country we don't know," he resumed. "In fact, until the other day we didn't know he was back. I happened to be standing in Piccadilly when along comes a fellow wearing an Eton tie looking like he'd bought the Ritz. His face rang a bell and I had another look at him. Then I got him, although I hadn't seen him for close on five years. It was the Toff—without the nifty little moustache he used to wear. He was looking so prosperous that I strolled along behind him to see whether he had really made good, or was still making bad. I found he was living in a little hotel in Bayswater under the name of Lancelot Seymour. Trust his nibs to pick on something fancy. This is him." The Inspector took a photograph from his pocket-book and laid it on Biggles's desk.

"You didn't pick him up?" queried Biggles, looking at the portrait.

"No. I could have asked him some awkward questions, no doubt, about how he got over here and what he was using for an identity card, ration book and so on; but we believe in giving a man a chance. All the same, I put a man on to try to spot the source of this sudden prosperity. How do you think the Toff was amusing himself?"

Biggles shook his head. "I'm no good at guessing. You tell me."

"He's learning to fly."

Biggles smiled.

"It's a fact," declared the Inspector. "He's a highly respected member of the Home Counties

Flying Club—all poshed up in cap and goggles, standing drinks to the boys and girls and generally doing the heavy."

Biggles's smile broadened.

"It's nothing to laugh about," protested the Inspector. "The Toff can really fly. I've made discreet enquiries and found he'd not only been solo, but had got his 'A' Licence. That ain't enough. It seems he has set his heart on becoming a regular commercial pilot, for which reason he's now working for the 'B' Licence. He spends most of his time at the club, and from the questions he asks he wants to know all there is to know about flying."

"Perhaps he *has* turned over a new leaf and is at last on his way to earn an honest living."

The Inspector shook his head sadly. "I'm afraid there's a wasp in that jar of jam, although so far I haven't been able to spot it. You see, when I knew he was back, I got in touch with police headquarters in Canada and asked them how the Toff had been behaving himself. Naturally we tipped them off when he went over there. How would you suppose his lordship had been occupying his time?"

"I've told you before. I'm no good at guessing."

"Learning to fly! Now think that one over," requested the Inspector with a grim sort of satisfaction. "Not only did he learn to fly, but he passed all his tests and was finally graded as a top-line pilot."

Biggles's face expressed astonishment. "I should never have guessed that one," he confessed. "So it boils down to this. Mr. Lancelot Seymour becomes a qualified pilot in Canada and then comes back to this country, joins a flying club, and says he wants to learn to fly."

"That's it. Doesn't it smell phoney to you?"

"It more than smells phoney to me," asserted Biggles. "I'd say it stinks."

"What's his idea, do you think?" asked the Inspector helplessly.

Biggles tapped a cigarette thoughtfully on the back of his hand. "We might make a lot of guesses and be wrong every time," he opined. "No doubt we shall learn the answer in due course."

"What's the use of that?" demanded the Inspector. "I want to know *now*, not after this wily bird has spread his wings and flown away with a golden worm in his beak."

"All right, let's look at it like this," said Biggles. "If this man is a qualified pilot then this learning to fly is a blind. For what purpose? There must be one, and I think it's fairly plain. Wanting to learn to fly was his reason for joining the club; and the reason why he wanted to join the club was to have access to aircraft should he need one in a hurry. Alternatively, he might want to use an aircraft for some purpose of his own—an improper purpose, of course. What puzzles me is his wanting a 'B' Licence. The

'A' Licence is all he needs to fly about solo. Wait a minute, though. I may have got something. In order to get a 'B' Licence a pupil has to make a cross-country flight—at night. On such a trip, if he disappeared for a little while nobody would be worried or even surprised because people would think—and he would no doubt say—he'd lost his way. That's a common enough occurrence. During his absence on a dark night he might do all sorts of things—go to all sorts of places. It might suit him one night to disappear entirely, then, after a while his death would be presumed, it being supposed that he'd gone into the sea. But we needn't go into that angle at the moment. I think it might be a good idea if I flew down to the Home Counties Aerodrome at Sudley and had a look at this smart dicky-bird, to see how his feathers are growing. Tell me this. Does the Toff specialise in any particular form of crime?"

"No. He's a sort of jack-of-all-trades. He's been a plain thief, a forger, a confidence trickster, a receiver of stolen goods and a black marketeer."

Biggles nodded. "A general practitioner, as you might say."

"His sort are a pain in the neck to the Force," grumbled the Inspector.

"I see. Well, give me a day or two to look at this fledgling night-hawk," requested Biggles. "I may have a quiet word with the club secretary at the same time. I know him well." He looked at his watch. "In fact, I'll slip down right away. Meanwhile, if anything turns up that looks like the Toff's work let me know."

"Okay," agreed the Inspector, getting up. "And if you get a line on him from your angle you might put me wise. Now I shall have to be getting back to the Yard. I'm still trying to trace that consignment of treasury notes that disappeared from the Euston– Crewe express the other night. Luckily the bank consigning them to one if its branches kept a record of the numbers, so that crooks who lifted them will have a job to get them into circulation without us spotting them."

Biggles walked with the Inspector to his car, which had been parked outside the hangar.

On the way back he called Ginger, who was working with Flight-Sergeant Smyth on one of the machines. "Get out No. 2 Auster," he ordered. "I'm not going far. You can come with me if you like."

"Good enough," acknowledged Ginger.

Half an hour later the Police Auster landed on the well-kept aerodrome of the Home Counties Flying Club, and taxying past two or three school machines that were standing on the tarmac came to rest near the clubhouse.

Biggles got out, took off his flying jacket, helmet

D

and goggles, and tossed them in his seat. Ginger did the same, and they walked together towards the veranda on which half a dozen members and an instructor were engaged in casual conversation. Hubert Gestner, alias Lancelot Seymour, was not among them, Biggles noticed, as with a nod he walked on into the lounge.

There he found the man in whom he was interested, on a high stool at the bar, talking to the barman. Having recognised him, Biggles barely glanced at him as he walked on to the office. After knocking, he put his head round the door, and smiled as he saw the man he was hoping to see, the club secretary, working at his desk. "Hallo, Tommy. How's things?" he greeted.

Ex-Flying Officer Tommy Clewson sprang to his feet. "Hallo, old timer! This is an unexpected treat. What lucky break brought you here? I heard you were——"

Biggles raised a warning finger and closed the door quickly. "Just forget for the moment anything you may have heard about me," he said softly.

The secretary's eyes opened wide. "You don't mean you've come here—on business?"

"I have," Biggles told him.

"Serious?"

"How serious remains to be seen. But there's no need to break into a perspiration. It's nothing to do with you personally. I want you, if you will, to answer one or two questions for me. Keep this under your hat, though, or you may start something. The reason I'm here is as much in your interest as mine. You've got a member under instruction named Seymour, I believe?"

"Yes. But you're not going to tell me that there's anything wrong with him?"

"There's nothing wrong with anybody, Tommy, until he's found out," murmured Biggles.

"But this chap, apart from being an apt pupil, is one of the most popular members we've ever had."

"He would be," returned Biggles evenly.

"Langley, his instructor, says he's the most brilliant pupil he's ever had in his hands. He swears he'll go far."

"He may one day go farther than Langley imagines," returned Biggles dryly. "He's got his 'A' ticket, I believe?"

"Went through like a bird."

"How long has he been a member here?"

"A couple of months or so."

"And I understand that he's now after his 'B' Licence?"

"He's almost got it. He has only one more test to pass."

"Must be a clever fellow," observed Biggles, mildly sarcastic.

"He might have been flying all his life," declared the secretary.

Biggles nodded. "When you said that you said more than you knew. What's this last test that's holding him up?"

"The cross-country night flight, solo. He tried it once and failed. Pity."

"A great pity," agreed Biggles. "But when was this?"

"About a week ago."

"What happened?"

"The run was from Lympne to Croydon, but he got off his track somewhere and was adrift for some time. His tanks were nearly dry when he got in, so he may have been lucky."

"You lost touch with him, apparently?"

"Yes."

"What explanation did he give?"

"He was quite frank about it. He said he'd run into some ground mist and lost his way."

"What are instruments for?"

Tommy shrugged.

Biggles went on. "I imagine he got a Met. report before he started—or his instructor should have got it for him; and no doubt someone checked his compass course. Was there any sudden change in the weather?"

"No—but you know how it is," protested Tommy. "Don't be hard on him. We all make mistakes at times."

"Between you and me he's made several mistakes

in his time—but don't let him see you know anything about that," returned Biggles. "Have arrangements been made yet for his next test?"

"As a matter of fact they have. He's trying again tonight, weather permitting."

"What's the course this time?"

"He's to fly from here to Lympne."

"At what time?"

"He starts at nine o'clock. No big machines are due in from the Continent at that hour so he won't be worried by the risk of anything crossing his track."

"Thanks, Tommy. That's all I want to know," said Biggles. "Don't be surprised if you see me hanging around about nine o'clock. Take no notice of me if you do, unless I speak to you. And whatever you do don't mention the word police between now and then. See you later."

"Here! Half a minute!" expostulated the secretary. "What's all this about?"

"I'll tell you tonight—that is, if I know myself," answered Biggles. "By the way, has Seymour a car?"

"Yes. He uses it to run between here and Town. Aren't you going to stay to lunch?"

"No thanks."

"Well, at least have a drink before you go?"

"No thanks." Biggles smiled. "Can't you see I'm working?"

"Okay," sighed Tommy. "Have it your own way. You always were a queer bird."

"I'm not the only queer bird in your little aviary," said Biggles smilingly as he went out.

At a quarter to nine the airfield was deserted except for two mechanics in overalls who were running up the engine of a machine that had just been pulled out of a lighted hanger. In the clubhouse itself only one or two members lingered at the bar. Biggles and Ginger stood on the veranda doing nothing in particular, and there, presently, the club secretary joined them.

"So there you are," he observed. "What are you looking at?"

"The weather," replied Biggles casually. "Beautiful night for a spot of moonlight aviation."

"Couldn't be better. Seymour should have no difficulty in getting through this time. He should even be able to make a safe landing should he get lost and run out of petrol."

"As you say, he should have no difficulty at all," murmured Biggles. "Where is he, by the way?"

"Getting into his kit. Ah! There he is now. That's Langley, his instructor, with him. Giving him a final word of advice, I imagine. The machine they're making for is the machine detailed for the job."

"How long has Langley been with you?"

"Five years. He's got a fine record. Naturally we checked up before we engaged him."

"I see." Biggles walked slowly along to the tarmac. "It's always interesting to see a fellow take off on a test flight," he observed casually.

Pupil and instructor, the former in flying kit, had by this time reached the machine allocated for the test, one of the club's Tiger Moths, and were standing by a wing, talking in cheerful tones. The two mechanics, who had retired a short distance, stood watching or waiting for orders. Biggles, Ginger and the club secretary walked to within a dozen paces and also halted as if to watch the machine take off.

For two or three minutes the position remained unchanged. Then the instructor looked at his watch and shook hands with his pupil. "Off you go and the best of luck," he said, and backed away.

Seymour turned to the cockpit as if to climb in; but at this juncture a man in chauffeur's uniform appeared from the direction of the car park and came hurrying across the concrete apron towards the machine. He carried a brown-paper parcel.

"Hi! Just a minute, sir," he called. "You forgot your pyjamas. You'll want them if you stay the night at Lympne."

"Who's that?" asked Biggles, in a low but terse voice.

"That's Seymour's driver," answered the secretary.

By this time Seymour had turned. "Oh, thank you, James—how careless of me," he said nonchalantly, as he reached for the parcel.

But Biggles, who had already started forward, intercepted it before either Seymour or his man could have realised what he was going to do. "I'd like to have a look at this if you don't mind," he said quietly.

There was a brief silence, the result, presumably, of surprise. Then Seymour said, in a voice brittle with resentment: "Give me that. What do you think you're doing?"

"You heard what I said," said Biggles imperturbably.

"You've got a nerve," cried Seymour indignantly. "That's my property. What's it got to do with you? Are you looking for trouble?"

"Possibly," returned Biggles.

Tension was now perceptible in the atmosphere. "Who are you?" demanded Seymour in a curious voice.

"We're police officers," Biggles told him. "I'm sorry to trouble you, but—stop that man!"

The chauffeur had decided not to wait. He turned to run, but Ginger put out a foot and tripped him so that he fell heavily, cursing. There was a quick scuffle, which ended when the two mechanics, on Biggles's instructions, went to Ginger's assistance. The chauffeur, muttering, was pulled to his feet.

Biggles, who had remained near Seymour, spoke quietly to him. "Don't let's have any more trouble."

"But what's all this about?" cried Seymour. "I'm on a test flight and I'm due off the ground." He made a grab at the parcel.

Biggles held him off. "All right, take it easy," he said shortly.

"I'll sue you for wrongful arrest," declared Seymour hotly.

"You haven't been arrested yet," Biggles pointed out. "Why are you getting so upset? I merely want to see what's in this parcel."

"You heard what my man said. It's my pyjamas."

"In that case you've nothing to worry about," averred Biggles. "Come over to the clubhouse and we'll make sure there hasn't been a mistake. It won't take a minute."

Seymour hesitated. "All right, I'll go without them," he decided at last.

"There's no need to do that," argued Biggles. "A couple of minutes one way or the other is neither here nor there."

"Well, let me get out of this flying kit," requested Seymour.

"No, no. Don't trouble," returned Biggles.

Ginger, who was following the argument, smiled as he realised the purpose of the request. Encumbered by heavy flying clothes Seymour could neither run nor fight, had either been his intention.

"Come on!" ordered Biggles crisply. "There's been enough bickering."

The whole party, which included the secretary and the instructor—looking more than slightly bewildered—moved slowly towards the clubhouse. Reaching it, Biggles led the way across the veranda into the lounge. He went no farther than the nearest table. On it he put the parcel. In a silence that was oppressive he took out his penknife, cut the string and pulled it off.

The silence was broken only by the rustle of paper as he stripped it off to disclose what appeared to be a small bale of white muslin. With slow deliberation he unrolled it, and then turned accusing eyes on Seymour as he held up a miniature parachute. "Do you normally throw your pyjamas overboard before you land?" he enquired coldly.

Seymour's face was bloodless, his lips a thin hard line.

Biggles continued to unwrap the parcel, and presently there came to light a canvas bag to which the parachute was attached. Again the penknife came into action. A swift tear and the bag fell open, so that its contents were strewn on the table. They were bundles of one-pound notes, tightly packed as they are issued to banks.

Biggles looked up. His eyes came to rest on Seymour's face. "This doesn't look like a suit of pyjamas to me," he said softly.

"All right, smart guy," sneered Seymour. "So what? It's my money."

"This money," corrected Biggles, "is the property of Barclay's Bank. It was stolen last week between Euston and Crewe. I happen to know the serial numbers. If you say it's yours perhaps you'll tell us how it got into your possession. We needn't ask what you were going to do with it. It isn't far from Lympne to the other side of the Channel."

Seymour swallowed. "I can explain," he blurted hoarsely.

"Not now," murmured Biggles. "Wait till you get to headquarters. Gestner, you're under arrest, and I think you'll find it hard to prove there's anything wrongful about it. All right, you can get out of that flying kit. You won't be needing it. Inspector Gaskin is in the office. You can talk to him on the way to London. Ginger, you might call him."

The following day Biggles was explaining the case to the Air Commodore. "It was a bit difficult," he pointed out. "Of course, I knew he was up to something, but I hadn't a clue as to what it was, so I had to take a chance. I daren't let him, or the parcel, out of my sight. I couldn't follow him; I should have lost him in the dark. He'd have gone straight to France, dropped the parcel to a pal waiting for it, and then landed at Lympne with another excuse about losing his way to account for being overdue. It wouldn't have taken him long to slip across the Channel, anyway. Once the notes were over the other side they would have disappeared for good. The chauffeur was in it, too. I suppose Gestner didn't want to walk about with all that money on him so he got his chauffeur to sit in the car until he was ready to take off. In the ordinary way there was no reason why it shouldn't have worked."

"The chauffeur happens to be Tod Mills," stated Inspector Gaskin, who was present. "We've been looking for him for months. One thing with another we can call it a good night's work."

THE CASE OF THE MURDERED
APPRENTICE

"'MORNING, Bigglesworth. You seem to be busy here." Air Commodore Raymond made the remark as he strolled into the Operations Room of the Special Air Police.

"Good morning, sir. Not so busy as we shall be, I'm afraid," replied Biggles, pulling up a chair for his chief.

"That's a gloomy outlook," stated the Air Commodore. "Have you a reason for taking such a depressing view?"

"I don't see how it can be otherwise," answered Biggles. He smiled wanly. "In fact, I'm thinking of making an application for more men and more machines."

The Air Commodore looked startled. "Would you mind explaining this sudden burst of pessimism?"

"Not at all," returned Biggles, without enthusiasm. "It rests on the fact that the preoccupation of almost everyone today is how to get more spending money with the least possible effort. Some people are still prepared to get it honestly or not at all, but there's an increasing number who are determined to get it, anyway. The trouble is, those who are only slightly crooked don't seem to realize that they are potential criminals. They reckon they're just the wise guys. The worst aspect of it is that their children see what's going on, and imagining it's smart, start little rackets on their own which lands them in Borstal. That's the simple answer to the spate of juvenile crime which is giving magistrates a headache, and will, when the little crooks grow into big ones, keep me working overtime. You won't cure that by making more laws or building more prisons. Keep the home clean and you keep the kids clean. That's the answer. Am I right?"

"So far," conceded the Air Commodore. "Go on."

"All right. Unfortunately it so happens that government regulations, intended to make life easier for the majority, have also had the effect of making things easier for those who aren't particular about how they get their money. For example: the value of a thing should depend on the law of supply and demand; but values are now fixed by officials, and as no two governments think alike the result is a tangle of false values. An article costing half a crown in France may be worth a pound over here. And vice versa. Consequently, in order to make money fast all you have to do is buy in one country and sell in another. In other words, the road to

Easy Street is merely a matter of transportation. You'll say steps have been taken to prevent such trading, and up to a point I'd agree with you. The illegal movement of merchandise, commonly called smuggling, is pretty well under control where ordinary surface transport is concerned; but there's still one vehicle which is difficult to stop, and that's the aeroplane, which is fast, independent of tides and timetables, and has all the space between heaven and earth in which to operate. The possibilities offered by aircraft are now being realized by the smart guys—and you ask me why I'm depressed! With machines able to cover fifty miles in five minutes it's now possible, for all practical purposes, for a man to be in two places at once. To keep pace I shall soon have to travel so fast that I shall meet myself coming back. The ground Force can't help. It takes an airman to catch an airman. Sorry to be so long-winded, but you asked for it."

The Air Commodore tapped the ash off his cigarette. "It's funny you should say that, because it's just such a case of a fellow being in two places at once that brought me here today."

Biggles shook his head sadly. "I should have known there was a trick in it. What's the latest miracle?"

"It won't take long to tell," asserted the Air Commodore. "Today is Monday. Yesterday, at twelve noon, an aircraft apprentice named Edmund Teale proceeded on leave from Halton Camp to his home near Buckbury, in Essex, where his father is a gamekeeper. Teale caught his train and arrived at Buckbury station last night at ten minutes to eleven, where he ascertained from the station-master that, as the train was late, he had missed the last bus to Stanfield Corner, which would have passed near his home. He did the natural thing. Leaving his kit-bag with the station-master, saying he would call for it next day, he took his haversack and started to walk. The distance by road to his home is six miles, but as there's a short cut across the fields that does it in four he took it. The station-master at Buckbury has confirmed that he last saw Teale on the footpath at eleven o'clock. The boy should have been home by midnight. He didn't arrive; and he never will, because at dawn this morning his dead body was picked up on the Dutch coast. An early bather saw a body on a sandbank. He fetched the coastguard who brought it in. The uniform and identity disc told the police who it was. They phoned the Air Ministry, who have asked me to investigate."

"And now you're asking me?"

"Exactly."

"Then let's make sure I've got my facts right. The boy was at Buckbury at eleven o'clock last night —that's definite?"

"Yes."

"And at what time was the body found?"

"Five o'clock this morning."

"Which means that, alive or dead, he had been transported from a footpath in Essex to Holland in six hours. That, in turn, means that he was carried in an aircraft."

"Obviously. The time factor rules out anything else."

"What was the cause of death—drowning?"

"No. The boy must have been dead when he was put in the water. There was no water in his lungs. He had been shot in the heart, from close range, by a bullet fired from a Luger automatic pistol. The bullet is now on its way to us by air."

"So we have a plain case of murder."

"There's no doubt about that," agreed the Air Commodore. "If we can find the owner of the Luger that fired the bullet that killed the boy we should have enough evidence for a conviction; but in the absence of any motive I'm afraid that's going to be difficult."

"I can't altogether agree with you there," said Biggles quietly. "There's always a motive for murder although it may not be instantly apparent."

"But what possible reason could anyone have for killing this unfortunate, harmless boy?"

"Unfortunate, yes, but not necessarily harmless," disputed Biggles. "But let us not argue about it. As far as material to work on is concerned I've enough to keep us busy for the rest of the day."

"I'm glad to hear you say it," murmured the Air Commodore, rising. "I'll leave you to it."

"Have Teale's parents been told yet?"

"They've had a wire to say the boy died in an accident. An officer is now on the way down to tell them as much as we know."

"Nobody else knows the details?"

"Not yet."

"What about the boy's haversack. Has it been found?"

"No."

Biggles stubbed his cigarette. "All right, sir. That's all I want to know. Believe you me, I shall try very hard to find the skunk who shot an unarmed boy. If I do find him we'll see what happens when he meets someone who also carries a pistol."

The Air Commodore nodded. "Let me know how you get on," were his last words.

The brief silence that followed the Air Commodore's departure was broken by Ginger, who had listened to the conversation from the map table where he had been working with Algy and Bertie. "From the way you spoke anyone would think the case bristled with clues," he observed. "I can't see one."

"That's because you don't look hard enough," bantered Biggles, reaching for another cigarette.

"Suppose you tell us, and save time," suggested Ginger.

"All right," agreed Biggles. "Let's start with the motive. There must be one. When that boy set out to walk home he was perfectly normal. The tragedy therefore occurred or began during the walk. He was shot. The person who shot him didn't do it for fun. He had a reason. What could it have been? Considering the circumstances there could only have been one, or possibly two. He wanted the boy out of the way or he wanted to silence a witness. The two things go together, because having silenced the boy he would have to get rid of the body, anyway. Why did this person find it necessary to silence the boy? Obviously because the boy had seen something, or learned something, during the course of his walk. For the sake of argument we can say that as Teale walked home he saw or heard something which engaged his attention. We might even say, his *professional* attention. After all, he was a budding airman, and, as we know, an aircraft comes into the picture. He investigated, and was killed—not by an ordinary weapon, mark you, but by a Luger pistol, which is something a man carries for just such a purpose for which it was used. Exactly where Teale was killed we don't know—yet. What we do know is, the murderer decided to dispose of the body by dropping it from an aircraft into the sea. By no other means could the body have reached the place where it was found. It follows, therefore, that the murderer had an aircraft available. It might not be stretching conjecture too far to say it was this aircraft which the boy saw, and going to look at it—as he certainly would—saw too much."

"But I still don't see how you're going to start looking for a man who, having flown to Holland, might now be anywhere in Europe," argued Ginger.

"Let's see what we now have to work on," suggested Biggles. "Indisputably, the boy boarded, or was carried aboard, an aircraft. As it isn't possible to board an aircraft in flight, it follows that between eleven o'clock and midnight last night an aircraft was standing on the ground near the path that runs from Buckbury to Stanfield Corner. It must have been near the path because, as it was dark, the boy wouldn't otherwise have seen it. He may have watched it land. In any case, he would know that only one of two reasons would cause a machine to land there. Either it had made a forced landing or else it was engaged in an illegal undertaking. We know it didn't make a forced landing because it was able to take off again and fly to Holland. The landing, therefore, must have been irregular, otherwise the machine would have touched down on an official Customs airport—particularly if it had a foreign registration, as seems not unlikely. My argument that the landing was improper is supported by the fact that the pilot carried a gun, which is something a respectable civil pilot has no need to carry. He was ready for trouble should it arise. It did arise, and he used it—from which we may judge the character of the man we're looking for. As the Luger is a continental weapon the chances are that he's a foreigner—possibly, as the machine went to Holland, a Dutchman."

"But are we quite sure that he went to Holland," put in Ginger. "He might have flown out to sea, dropped the boy, and come back."

"It wouldn't have been necessary for him to fly right across the North Sea simply to dispose of the body," declared Biggles. "One part of the sea would have been as good as another for that purpose. As the machine crossed the sea we may suppose it's still there, because having been to the trouble to make a night flight it's hardly likely that the pilot would fly back in broad daylight—particularly after doing what he had done, knowing that he would be seen. Anyway, for a start let's look at the place where the thing began. It shouldn't be difficult to find, because in the short distance between Buckbury and the keeper's cottage there can't be many places big enough for a machine to make a landing—a night landing, at that. Fetch the six-inch Ordnance

Survey map of the district." Biggles got up and walked over to the map table.

Ginger brought the map and opened it on the table.

The point of Biggles's pencil descended on Buckbury. "Here we are," he said. "Here's Buckbury. Here's the path. This is better than I could have hoped for. See what I mean? The path runs through timbered parkland for more than half the way. There could be no landing there. Here's a big field, though—the only one as far as I can see. It seems to be on the estate of this place, Larford Hall. All right. That's as much as we shall learn from the map. Algy, slip down in the Auster with Bertie and get me a strip of vertical photos from two thousand. Cover the whole length of the path while you're at it. Be as quick as you can. I'll make some phone calls while you're away. Ginger, ring up headquarters Essex Constabulary; find out the name of the police officer at Buckbury and get him on the phone."

Ginger turned to the instrument while Biggles had another look at the map.

Within five minutes Ginger had the required information, and passed Biggles the receiver. "Here you are," he said quietly. "Sergeant Winskip is the name."

Biggles, note-book beside him and pencil in hand, took over. "Good morning, Sergeant. This is

Bigglesworth of Scotland Yard here. I want you to answer a question or two. I believe you have a biggish place on your beat called Larford Hall . . . that's right. Who lives there now? . . . Mrs. Vanester. Came here from Paris. Dutch lady originally from Java . . . ah-huh. How long has she had Larford Hall? . . . Twelve months. Has a business in London, eh. What sort of business? . . . High-class milliner in Bond Street. Trades under the name of Madame Karena. Yes, I've got that. Now tell me, have you had any complaints lately about low flying? . . . You haven't. What's the name of the postmaster at Buckbury? . . . Mr. Green. Right, Sergeant. That's all. Thank you. Goodbye." Biggles hung up and looked at his watch. "We've just time to run up to Bond Street before Algy gets back and develops his photos. Get the car."

Ginger hesitated. "What the dickens are you expecting to see in Bond Street?"

"You heard my conversation with the sergeant," asserted Biggles. "I'm going to glance at Madame Karena's bonnet shop."

"What do you expect to see there?"

"Hats, of course."

"*Hats!*" Ginger looked incredulous. "What have hats got to do with us?"

"That's just what I'm wondering," said Biggles softly. "Of course, these are ladies' hats—very expensive, no doubt."

"So what?"

"I imagine expensive hats **have expensive** decorations."

"Such as?"

"Well, feathers, for instance."

"Are you kidding?"

"This is no kidding matter, my lad. Judging from what a fellow working for Guinea Airways once told me, when I had occasion to call at New Guinea, the feathers that once made fine birds can also make fat bank balances. Let's go and see."

Half an hour later Biggles's car glided in to the kerb outside a small but expensive-looking establishment over which, in flowing letters of gold, appeared the name Madame Karena. There was only one window. Behind it, on a stand, was displayed one article. It was a hat, a small hat from which sprang two curving plumes, one up, one down. No price was marked.

"Let's go in and see what they want for that flimsy piece of frivolity," suggested Biggles.

He led the way in. To an elegant young lady who came forward he said: "A friend of mine has asked me to find out the price of the hat you have in the window."

"The price is fifty guineas, sir," was the reply.

"Thank you, but I'm afraid that's rather more than I thought," said Biggles sadly.

"Ragianas are very rare now, sir, but we have

others," said the girl, raising a hand to where more hats were on view—mostly, Ginger noticed, trimmed with gorgeous feathers.

"I was only interested in the one in the window," replied Biggles. "By the way, are you by any chance Madame Karena?"

"No, sir. Madame Karena seldom comes to the shop. She designs our models at home."

"I see. Thank you. Good morning." Biggles went out and back to the car.

"Fifty guineas," breathed Ginger. "Stiffen the skylarks! Women must be crazy. Ten fivers and then some for a couple of twirls of fluff. The hen they grew on must have been hatched from the original golden egg."

"You may be nearer the mark than you imagine," Biggles told him. "Those bits of fluff, as you call them, are worth considerably more than their weight in gold."

"I still don't get it," muttered Ginger helplessly, as Biggles started the car.

"That's because you don't read the right sort of books," murmured Biggles, smiling. "You heard what I told the Air Commodore this morning. It's all a matter of supply and demand. Those feathers don't grow on barn-yard hens, laddie."

"What do they grow on?"

"A fool of a fowl that so dolls itself up with finery to dazzle its girl friends that it's known as the Bird of Paradise. I call it a fool because all it usually gets for its trouble is a twisted neck. It's been hunted almost to extinction by plumage poachers—poachers because the wretched bird is now strictly protected by law; anyway in British territory."

"The girl called them Ragianas—or something."

"Ragianas are one of several species. Others, I remember, are called Magnificents, Superbs, Gorgets and Empresses. Some time ago, when I was in New Guinea, they were the main topic of conversation on account of the new prohibition law. The punishment for bumping off one of those gorgeous birdies was pretty severe, too. A fine of two hundred pounds and up to two years' imprisonment. Did that stop it? Not on your life. All it did was boost the value of the feathers sky high, so that poaching became even more profitable. The more rare the bird, the more expensive its feathers. The more expensive the feathers the rarer the bird becomes. That's how it goes with everything today. The moral is, don't cock your tail too high or you're liable to lose it."

"But what in thunder has all this to do with us," cried Ginger.

"I'll give you a line on the way it begins to look to me," answered Biggles. "The Bird of Paradise dwells, as a matter of unromantic fact, in the jungles of the East Indies—notably New Guinea. The East Indies are mostly Dutch. Madame Karena came

from Java which is in the Dutch East Indies—or
Indonesia, as they call it now. As you may have
noticed, she isn't short of Paradise plumes. How
does she get them? I can't think they come through
our Customs because we've made it illegal to kill the
bird. Anyway, the duty would be enormous.
Dutch aircraft operate to and from the East Indies,
so it wouldn't be surprising if there were plumes
available in Holland. Last night an aircraft landed
near Madame Karena's country house. As it later
flew to Holland we might assume it came from there.
I don't know what it brought here, but it certainly
brought something; and as Madame Karena is well
supplied with decorations for her fabulous titfers it
might well be that the plane brought her some, which
might not have got in through ordinary channels,
and would have to pay a fantastic duty if they did.
Anyhow, that's how it begins to look to me."

"And me, now you've been kind enough to give
me the gen," said Ginger.

Algy was waiting with the photographs when they
got back to the airfield, the prints, still damp, having
been arranged as a single picture on the table.
Biggles picked up a large magnifying glass and
subjected them to a searching scrutiny.

"Okay," he said at last. "These tell us all we
really wanted to know. There's only one place
within easy distance of the footpath where an

orthodox aircraft could land, and that's the big field in front of Larford Hall. As a path leads to it from the house it's evidently part of the estate. Having seen it from topsides' we'll now go down and have a worm's-eye view."

"Do you mean fly down?" asked Ginger.

"Not likely. That might scare somebody. We'll go down by car. There's no great hurry."

"What beats me is this," averred Ginger. "If the bloke we're looking for is in Holland how are we going to get at him?"

"With any luck we might arrange for him to come over to us," answered Biggles blandly.

"But that may mean hanging about the field night after night for weeks, on the off-chance of him coming over," said Ginger, aghast.

"Not necessarily," corrected Biggles. "If we whistle he may come back tonight. Algy, I'm afraid you'll have to take over here while I'm away." As he spoke, Biggles took an automatic from the drawer of his desk, loaded it and put it in his pocket. "Bring your guns," he told Ginger and Bertie. "We're dealing with a man who not only packs a pistol but is ready to use it—even on a kid. Well, if he tries it on me he'll find me ready."

Three hours later, having had lunch on the way, Biggles brought the car to a stop outside the village post office at Buckbury. Inside, they found the postmaster busy behind the counter.

"Mr. Green?" queried Biggles.

"Yes."

Biggles showed his police badge. "I'm from Scotland Yard and I want a word with you," he said quietly. "In fact, I may need your co-operation."

The postmaster looked alarmed until Biggles reassured him. "There's nothing for you to worry about," he told him. "Am I right in supposing that Larford Hall comes in your postal area?"

"Yes."

"You handle the letters to and from the Hall."

"Yes. Mrs. Vanester often comes here herself."

"What sort of woman is she? I mean, how does she strike you?"

"All right. She doesn't say much. I'd put her age at about forty. She's on the big side, and good-looking in a foreign sort of way. I don't think she's altogether European, although that's only my opinion."

"I believe she says she's Dutch."

"That's right. She often sends letters to Holland."

"You see her mail, then?"

"Of course."

"Who does she write to in Holland?"

"Usually it's to one address."

"Can you remember it?"

"I've seen it enough times. She writes to Mr. Rudolf Lurgens. His address is Rossenhalle, near Hillegom, Holland."

"Does she ever send cablegrams to him?"

"She has, once or twice."

"How does she usually sign herself?"

"Karena. That's her Christian name, I believe."

"I see. Give me a telegram form," requested Biggles. "I want to send a cable to the same address."

The postmaster looked surprised, but made no comment. He put a form on the counter. Biggles picked up a pen, and Ginger, looking over his shoulder, saw him write, after the address: "Return tonight without fail. Important new business." He signed it "Karena".

"You can get that off as soon as you like," ordered Biggles, handing back the form. "Is Mrs. Vanester on the phone?"

"Yes. The number is Buckbury 401."

"Her calls come through your switchboard?"

"Yes."

"Will you be on duty yourself for the rest of the day?"

"Yes."

"Good. Unless I ring up myself, personally, I want you to block all calls to and from Larford Hall until further notice. Say the line's out of order— make any excuse you like. Can you do that?"

"If those are police orders, yes."

"All right. Not a word of this to anyone, you understand?"

"You can rely on me," said the postmaster. "Excuse me asking, but is this anything to do with Mrs. Teale's boy, who was——?"

"What do you know about that?" asked Biggles sharply.

"I had to deliver the telegram saying he had been killed."

"Ah, of course," replied Biggles. "Yes, that's it, but keep quiet about it."

"I'll keep quiet," promised the postmaster grimly. "Eddy was a nice boy. I've known him since he was a toddler."

Biggles went out. "Now I think we'll park the car and have a cup of tea while we have the chance. Then we'll take a stroll along the footpath to see what we can find there."

"Do you think this man Lurgens is the man we're looking for?" asked Ginger.

"He might be," answered Biggles. "I took a chance on it. If it isn't we've done no harm."

Twilight was closing in by the time they had reached that part of the footpath that fringed the grounds of Larford Hall, a large red-brick house, sections of which could be seen through the trees. So far the path had traversed wooded country, but now, while timber persisted on one side, the other lay open to the big grass field in which, if Biggles's reasoning had been correct, the apprentice had lost his life. Entrance to this field was, however, barred by a fence of formidable appearance. The lower four feet comprised tightly-stretched, square-meshed sheep wire. Above this ran three strands of barbed wire.

"Someone has been to some trouble to keep people out of the field, anyway," observed Biggles.

Ginger pointed to a notice. "Beware of the bull," he read. "That may be the reason."

"As you say, it may be the reason—but I doubt it," answered Biggles. "Such signs can be an old trick to discourage trespassers. I don't see any bull, anyway." He walked on slowly, examining the wire as he went.

"Are you looking for something?" asked Ginger presently.

"Yes, I'm looking for the place where the boy got over," returned Biggles. "It shouldn't be hard to find. He could hardly have climbed up that mesh without bending the wire that carried his weight. Ah! This looks like it." He pointed to a section of wire that had been bent in the manner he had suggested. Speaking to Ginger, he went on: "If you were walking along here, carrying a haversack, and suddenly decided to climb the fence, what's the first thing you'd do?"

"Dump the haversack."

"I'd think that, too," agreed Biggles. "The boy's haversack shouldn't be far away."

Bertie stooped and lifted something from the bracken almost at his feet. "Here it is, poor little beggar," he said quietly.

"Leave it where it is for the moment," ordered Biggles. "This, then, is where he got over. Which means that the aircraft must have been standing just inside the field, or he wouldn't have seen it. He must have wondered, not without reason, what it was doing there, and, deciding to find out, he got shot for his pains. Stand fast, you two. I'm going over."

The others watched him climb the fence, walk a little way into the field and then quarter the area slowly. He stopped, looking at something on the ground. Then he stopped, picked up an object in his handkerchief and rejoined those on the path. "I was right," he said. "That's where the machine stood. She dripped a little oil out of the engine, as they usually do."

"What did you pick up?" asked Ginger.

Biggles opened his handkerchief. "The case of the cartridge that killed Teale. The automatic ejected it after the shot. Being dark, the man who fired it couldn't find it—or didn't bother. We're getting on."

"And now what's the drill, old boy?" asked Bertie.

E

"The drill is, as there's nothing more we can do for the moment, I'm going to sit down and have a quiet cigarette for a little while. Then Ginger will come with me as a witness while I have a word with Mrs. Vanester. Bertie, you'll stay here. If the machine lands, do nothing until the pilot has gone to the house, as I think he will. Then your job will be to see that the machine doesn't leave the ground again." Biggles looked at the sky. "It's a fine night, anyway," he remarked inconsequently.

It was ten o'clock when, with Ginger beside him, he rang the front-door bell of Larford Hall. It was answered by a butler. "I'd like to see Mrs. Vanester on a personal matter of importance," Biggles told him.

They were invited into a hall, where the butler left them, presently to return and conduct them to a well-furnished sitting-room of some size. A tall, dark, heavily built but good-looking woman of middle age rose from a chair where she had been at work, apparently making a hat.

"Good evening. You have something to say to me?" she questioned, speaking with a pronounced accent.

"Yes," replied Biggles. "I fear I am the bearer of bad news. We're from police headquarters."

The woman did not move or speak, but Ginger, who was beginning to know the signs of nervous emotion, saw the end of her nose turn white.

"Is Mr. Lurgens, of Rossenhalle, Holland, a relation of yours?" asked Biggles.

Mrs. Vanester's hand flew to her heart. "He is my brother!" she cried. "Don't tell me he has crashed? Always I feared that he would fall in his aeroplane and be killed."

"I didn't say anything about an aeroplane," returned Biggles quietly. "But while we are on the subject, will you tell me why he found it necessary to land here last night instead of at an official airport? I have warned you that we are police officers."

For a moment the woman did not answer. She stared at Biggles as if his face fascinated her. "Who said he landed here?" she asked at last, in a curious strained voice.

"I did," replied Biggles evenly. "I asked you *why* he landed."

"He wanted to see me, of course. Why not?"

"As you say, why not? But why land here? Why not land at the proper place?"

The woman shrugged. "I know nothing about flying."

"I suggest that he landed here because he carried something he did not want to declare to the Customs officers."

"Such nonsense!" scoffed the woman. "He brought nothing but a small present for me."

"Would you call the box of feathers which I see

on the floor beside your chair a small present?" inquired Biggles.

The woman drew a deep breath. "Very well!" she exclaimed curtly. "What of it? What are a few feathers? Is the possession of feathers a crime?"

"That depends on the feathers and how they were brought here," replied Biggles.

"So!" challenged the woman haughtily. "If there is a duty to pay I will pay it."

Biggles shook his head. "You cannot, Mrs. Vanester, evade the law in this country and gloss over it as easily as that."

"Well, what are you going to do about it?"

"I'm hoping to discuss that with your brother."

"That is impossible. He is in Holland."

"On the contrary, I think I hear him landing now," averred Biggles imperturbably.

For the first time the woman looked shaken. "Is he mad?" she muttered. "What could have brought him here?"

"I took the liberty of suggesting that you were anxious to see him."

"But I don't want to see him."

"No, but I do," said Biggles softly. "Here he is now, I think."

The door was thrown open, and a swarthy man, with an unstrapped flying helmet on his head and a leather jacket on his arm, strode into the room. After a swift glance at the two men he looked at the woman and said tersely: "What is this? Why do you ask me to come back?"

With a hand resting on his hip, Biggles answered. "Your sister didn't ask you to come back. I sent the telegram. I am a police inspector and I arrest you for the murder of Edmund Teale, an aircraft apprentice, outside this house last night. I must warn you that anything you say——"

The accused man did not say anything. But he acted—swiftly. The flying jacket fell from his arm as his hand flashed to his pocket. Biggles moved just as fast. Two shots crashed almost as one, making the lights jump. Silence fell. Pale blue cordite smoke reeked across the room. Biggles swayed a little on his feet, then stood still, his lips a thin line, a smoking pistol still half raised. The man facing him stretched out a hand for the table. His eyes, wide open, were on Biggles's face. His pistol fell with a soft thud on the carpet. Then, like a coat slipping from a peg, he crumpled in a heap on the floor.

The woman screamed, stumbled to a settee and collapsed on it.

Said Biggles, slowly and deliberately: "He asked for it. Ginger, pick up that gun. The phone's over there. Call Sergeant Winskip. Tell him he'll need an ambulance. Give my name to the operator or you may not get through." Then he walked stiffly to a chair and sat down.

Thus ended dramatically the case of the murdered apprentice. Lurgens, already wanted for murder, had nothing to lose by shooting at Biggles, who, realising this, was ready. Both shots took effect. Lurgen's shot hit Biggles in the side, making a flesh wound that put him in hospital for a week. Biggles's bullet did not kill Lurgens. It lodged in his body and was successfully removed. He was in hospital, on the way to recovery, when he made a desperate attempt to escape, tearing the stitches in his wound and causing complications from which he died a fortnight later.

Mrs. Vanester was deported as an undesirable alien.

Later it was revealed that Lurgens had once been employed as a pilot by a Dutch air-line company operating in Indonesia, and had been discharged for the very offence that in the end cost him his life. Ironically, the feathers that provided such a vital clue must have been only a sideline, judging from the big stocks of contraband goods found in Larford Hall, and black-market British currency found by the Dutch police in his house in Holland.

Exactly how Apprentice Teale met his death was never known, although it was proved by ballistic experts that Lurgens' pistol had fired the fatal shot. The probable explanation, supported by blood-stains in Lurgens' Fokker, was that Teale, on his way home, had seen the machine standing in the field, and, investigating, hit on the truth. Anyway, the smuggler had shot him and disposed of the body in a manner which he had every reason to suppose would be simple and safe. It may have been simple, but, as events proved, it was not safe. The body, from the lonely sandbank on which it fell, called for justice, and it did not call in vain.

THE CASE OF THE STOLEN AIRCRAFT

"IN MY time I've seen and heard so many surprising things that I've often told myself that nothing could ever surprise me again." Biggles smiled whimsically as, sitting in his room at the Operations Headquarters of the Air Police at Gatwick Airport, he reached for a cigarette.

"What is it this time, old warrior?" enquired Bertie, adjusting his monocle.

Biggles looked across at the map table on which Algy and Ginger were plotting a course. "Come here and listen to this," he requested.

"Have you just come from the Yard?" asked Algy, as he walked over.

"Yes. I found Wing Commander Lyall, Provost-Marshal of the R.A.F., there with the Air Commodore; and he told us as queer a yarn as I ever heard in my life, I think. I got a laugh out of it, too."

"Shoot away," demanded Algy.

"Follow the story closely and don't miss a word," said Biggles. "Here we go. Some time ago a pupil at the R.A.F. Training Establishment at Marling Road, in Suffolk, was detailed to do a cross-country test in a certain aircraft—to be precise, a Lysander numbered K.8009. Half an hour later, sweating in his flying kit, he returned to the Flight Office to say that he couldn't find the machine anywhere. Other people, including the Station Commandant, started looking, and they couldn't find it, either. In short, K.8009 wasn't on the airfield. Where was it? Nobody knew. Records showed that it had been overhauled and refuelled three days earlier and pulled out onto the concrete. With what reluctance we can well imagine the Station Commander had no alternative than to report to the Air Ministry that he had mislaid one perfectly good aircraft." Biggles stubbed his cigarette.

"A day or two after receiving this report the Air Ministry did the obvious thing. They sent a signal to all stations asking for a check to be carried out to see if anyone had an aircraft surplus to establishment. It was just possible that some thoughtless fellow had flown the machine to another airfield and forgotten to bring it back—a most unlikely proceeding, we must admit, but it was the only solution the Air House could think of. The check was carried out according to orders, but, far from producing the missing machine, another Station Commander, at another training unit, had to confess that he was one short. He had lost a perfectly good Mosquito, of all things. At any rate, it wasn't on the airfield. Nor could its absence be accounted for.

"Upon receiving this information the Air Council

became exceedingly wrathful, and Station Commanders up and down the country began to lose their beauty sleep. The R.A.F. started looking for its lost sheep, but they were not to be found. About this time somebody remembered that just before the scare started someone had rung up to say that, while out shooting grouse on the Yorkshire moors, he had come upon the wreckage of an aeroplane. He thought the Air Ministry might like to know about it. Nobody had paid much attention to this at the time because war-time wreckage is still lying about the more desolate parts of the country, and nobody had been reported missing, anyway. However, somebody was sent along to have a look at this particular mess. And, sure enough, it turned out to be the bits and pieces of Lysander K.8009. It had obviously gone into the ground flat-out, nose first, and scattered itself all over the landscape. Apparently it was flying itself at the time. At all events there was nobody in it or near it. How could you account for that?"

"The pilot, knowing he was going to collide with the floor, had already baled out," offered Ginger.

"Correct," answered Biggles. "That's the only possible answer. But who was he? Where was he going? What was he doing? Why didn't he report the accident? If something had gone wrong he would have been justified in stepping out."

Nobody answered.

"There is more to come," resumed Biggles. "The next step in this chain of curious events was a letter sent to the Air Ministry by a farmer in Lincolnshire. Very politely he asked them to remove the aeroplane that was standing in one of his fields as his cattle were using it as a rubbing post and he was afraid this wasn't doing it any good. An officer was sent along. What did he find?"

"The missing Mosquito," replied Bertie promptly.

Biggles nodded approvingly. "There are moments, Bertie, when your perception amounts almost to genius," he declared with gentle sarcasm. "You're quite right. There stood the lost Mosquito with hens roosting on it and a cart-horse scratching its tail on the rudder. How it got there nobody knows. The farmer swears he woke up one morning and found it there. But wait a minute. A very odd circumstance now arose. Records showed that just before the aircraft disappeared its tanks had been topped up ready for a long flight. When it was found the tanks were practically dry. That is to say, when the Mosquito left the ground it carried rather more than five hundred gallons of juice, which would give it a range of well over two thousand miles. Yet here it was, with almost empty tanks, within forty miles of the place where it started from. What do you make of that?"

"Nothing," said Bertie helplessly. "Absolutely nothing."

"I thought you wouldn't," murmured Biggles softly.

"Are there no pilots missing?" asked Ginger.

"Not one," answered Biggles.

"What I want to know," put in Algy, "is what happened to all the petrol? Did the pilot fly round and round for hours and hours until he'd used it all up?"

Biggles shook his head slowly. "That doesn't sound to me like the answer."

"But I say, look here, old boy; what does all this add up to—if you see what I mean?" asked Bertie.

"It doesn't add up to anything that makes sense," replied Biggles.

"And where do we come in?" enquired Ginger.

"We don't," Biggles told him. "At least, that is, not officially. The Air Ministry, as a matter of course, has now informed the Yard of these queer goings-on. I happened to be with Raymond and so heard about them. The Air Ministry has, I gather, confessed itself beaten, so if we can find the answers it should be a feather in the Air Commodore's cap. On the face of it the case is odd rather than sinister, but in aviation one never knows what lies behind a thing, however simple it may look. Until the mystery is solved it's impossible to say which government departments may be affected. It might be a matter of simple smuggling for Customs and Excise; it might be an ordinary police court job;

but it might just as well come within the province of the National Security Office. If the aircraft had disappeared entirely the thing wouldn't be so strange. One would suppose that the machines had been pinched by some bloke for purposes of his own, possibly for sale abroad. That has been done. But why pinch an aircraft and then throw it away? That's the nut we've got to crack."

"Where are you going to start looking for the answers?" asked Ginger.

"You tell me," invited Biggles. "It should provide you with a nice mental exercise."

"What's the Air Ministry doing about it?" demanded Bertie.

"Nothing, except that all stations have been ordered to watch their aircraft to make sure that the thing doesn't happen again; which is going to be no joke for the airmen who are going to lose half their sleep doing guard duty."

"Could this be the work of some bloke in the service having a joke—if you get my meaning?" asked Bertie.

"I wouldn't call pinching government property to the tune of £50,000 a joke," protested Biggles. "Neither will the fellow concerned, if he's caught at it," he added grimly.

"Could it be someone with a grievance, going this way to get his own back?" suggested Ginger.

"What satisfaction could he get out of that?"

enquired Biggles. "The only man to suffer at the finish is the tax-payer, who has to pay for the machines."

"I don't see how you're going to get to the bottom of it," observed Algy gloomily.

"Why not?"

"Well, by now the scent is stone-cold. You can't watch every machine in the country. As far as the machines already stolen are concerned—well, an aircraft doesn't leave tracks."

"Doesn't it?" asked Biggles blandly.

"Are you telling us you hope to find the bloke who pinched these machines?" enquired Bertie dubiously.

"Hope is the word."

"But how are you going to pick up his trail?"

"That's what I'd like you to tell me," replied Biggles evenly. "Think it over." He got up. "Ginger, tell Flight-Sergeant Smyth that I shall want the Auster ready to take off at the crack of dawn tomorrow morning. You can come with me if you like."

Ginger looked puzzled. "Is this anything to do with the case you've been talking about?"

"Of course."

"What are you going to look for?"

"The man who purloined the machines."

Ginger became slightly satirical. "Are you expecting to run into him in the atmosphere?"

"No, although there's just a chance of it. It's

more likely that I shall see him on the ground," answered Biggles, smiling.

"Are you kidding?"

"No."

"You really expect to see him?"

"I do."

"Then you know something?"

"I've got an idea."

"What is it?"

Biggles shook his head, a faint smile hovering about the corners of his mouth. "I've told you what Raymond told me. Work it out for yourself. It's time you skyway coppers did your own thinking."

Ginger looked hurt. "Well, give us a clue."

Biggles's smile broadened. "All right. Bring me a six-inch Ordnance Survey map of south Norfolk."

Ginger brought the sheet and unrolled it on Biggles's desk.

Biggles touched a spot with the point of a pencil. "That's where we're going," he said. "I expect to meet the bloke who pinched the planes. That's as much as I'm going to tell you. If he isn't there I shall be very disappointed."

The stars were paling in the sky when, the following morning, the Auster left the ground, and headed north with Biggles at the controls. Ginger, feeling rather chilly, for the early morning air was keen, after the metropolis had been skirted had nothing to do but gaze down at the still sleeping countryside. The tangle of roads that would soon be humming with traffic were still deserted; an occasional lorry on a main highway was the only thing that moved. For the rest, the scene was the flat, multi-coloured, patchwork quilt that every pilot soon gets to know so well. The weather was fair after a soft autumn night, and except for a little mist persisting over low ground visibility was good. Above, a few flecks of cloud, far to the west, were the only stains in an otherwise cloudless sky. In short, the conditions for flying were perfect.

For rather more than half an hour not a word was spoken, although Ginger, with a map on his knees, followed the course until Suffolk lay below them to the right, and Cambridgeshire, with the imposing cathedral of Ely conspicuous slightly ahead, to the left.

The engine cut suddenly, picked up, went on again, cut again, and then continued with an uneven note. The machine lost height.

Ginger, of course, assumed that the power unit was failing, and was about to make a remark to that effect when he saw Biggles's hand moving the throttle. Instead of saying what he was going to say, he remarked sharply: "What the dickens are you doing?"

"I am afraid we may be going to have a spot of engine trouble," answered Biggles, smiling curiously. "We may have a forced landing."

"What do you mean—are we going down or aren't we?"

"I shall go down when I see what I'm expecting to see," replied Biggles. "That should happen at any moment. I'm hoping to create the impression to anyone on the ground that we're having a spot of bother, which would account for a landing outside an authorised airfield."

"What are you looking for?"

"Wheel tracks on a big field. With the dew still on the ground they should be easy enough to see. In particular, I'm interested in tracks that fade away, as if the vehicle that made them——"

"Had taken wing."

"Exactly. You see the farm ahead, to the left and some distance from the road? There's a village a mile or so to the north of it."

"Yes."

"That's where I'm expecting to see the tracks. There are some nice big fields, anyway."

A minute later Ginger cried, in a voice in which surprise and satisfaction were blended: "Okay, there they are!"

"I've got them," returned Biggles.

The engine, which had been running unevenly, cut abruptly. The nose of the machine went down and the aircraft began a series of S turns that took it ever nearer to a large grass field across which ran several sets of parallel lines, some, curiously enough, beginning and some ending in the middle of the field for no apparent reason. In one corner of the field stood a farm with extensive outbuildings. Ginger thought he saw a movement there, but he was not sure.

The Auster landed, and with the engine running in short bursts ran on towards the farm. But before reaching it the airscrew stopped and the machine came to a standstill. Almost at once a man dressed in overalls left the building and came hurrying towards it.

"Be very careful," said Biggles as they got out. "I fancy this is the man I expected to see, but what sort of fellow he is I haven't the remotest idea. He may be dangerous or he may not."

The man turned out to be quite young—about twenty-five Ginger judged him to be. As soon as he was within speaking distance he called: "Pretty landing. I heard you having a spot of trouble." Which, as Biggles later remarked, at once betrayed an association with aircraft.

"Nothing serious, I think," returned Biggles casually.

"Bring her over to my sheds and I'll soon put her right," offered the man.

Biggles looked at him. "You talk as though you'd got a workshop there."

"I have," was the reply.

"Let's have a look at it," suggested Biggles.

"Come on." Without the slightest hesitation the man led the way towards the sheds, with Biggles and Ginger following close behind.

Ginger was prepared for almost anything, but he certainly was not prepared for the sight that met his eyes when the man pushed open some double doors and entered what was nothing less than a small aircraft factory. Most of the floor space was occupied by an aircraft, a light machine built on such unorthodox lines that Ginger could only stare at it in astonishment.

"What do you call this?" Biggles asked the man, inclining his head towards the machine.

"This," answered the man, with obvious pride, "is my own idea. The Lutton Flivver-plane, the machine that everyone will soon be flying. Only finished it a day or two ago. All I need now is someone to finance it and put it on the market. Are you interested?"

"Have you tested her yet?" asked Biggles.

"Up to a point. Taxi-ing tests were okay. I gave her a short run this morning. There are one or two teething troubles, but that was only to be expected. I'll soon put them right."

"If you ask me," said Biggles slowly, "I'd say that thing's a death-trap."

The man's expression changed. "Why?" he challenged.

"From what I can see standing here your aspect

ratio is cockeye; your centre of gravity is too far back
and the view forward is poor."

"Rot!" cried the man indignantly. "I'm not
asking you to fly it," he added rather rudely.

"I wouldn't, at a gift," Biggles assured him
frankly. He looked around. "You've got a nice lot
of equipment here. Must have cost quite a lot of
money."

"It did."

"Some of it looks like service stuff."

"I got it from the Disposals people."

Biggles nodded. "I thought that pneumatic drill
you've got over there was still in short supply in the
R.A.F."

"They let me have one, anyhow," muttered the
man in a surly voice.

"What do you use for petrol, if it isn't a difficult
question to answer?" asked Biggles evenly.

"I know how to get what I want," retorted the
man. "I can get all the petrol I need."

"From where?" asked Biggles smoothly.

For the first time the man hesitated. Suspicion
flashed in his eyes. "What do you want to know for?"
he demanded in a queer voice.

"I have an interest, that's all," answered Biggles.

"In what way?"

"Because, Lutton," replied Biggles slowly, "we
happen to be police officers. I'm trying to locate
the petrol that was taken from two service aircraft

stolen a little while ago. I think I've found it. Am I right?"

The face of the man addressed had turned as white as paper. His tongue flicked over his lips. Then he moved suddenly. His hand went to a bench behind him and came forward holding a revolver. He covered Biggles with it.

Biggles didn't move. "Don't be a fool, Lutton," he said calmly. "Threatening a police officer in this country is a serious matter. You'll only make your case worse. I'll forget it happened if you'll put that thing away."

For a moment Lutton remained undecided, his eyes on Biggles's face. Then he drew a deep breath. "I suppose you're right," he said bitterly, and tossed the revolver back on the bench. "Well, what are you going to do about it?" he asked harshly.

"For the moment, nothing," replied Biggles. "I shall of course report the matter but after that the thing will pass out of my hands. If you take my advice you'll just stay here quietly and take what's coming to you. That's all." With that he turned away, and, followed by Ginger, walked back to the Auster without a word.

He climbed into his seat and took off.

An hour later he was back in his office. He went straight to the telephone and put a call through to the Air Commodore.

"You can tell the Air Ministry that the man who

lifted the two aircraft is Merville Lucas Lutton, of Wimbold Farm, near Methwold, Norfolk," he reported. "You'll find most of the petrol there, I think."

Half an hour later, after some breakfast, Biggles sat at his desk with the others demanding to be told how he had so quickly picked up a scent that had led straight to the heart of what looked like a first-class mystery.

Biggles reached for a cigarette. "Take it easy and I'll tell you. Really, it was all very simple.

"I may be wrong," he went on, "but it has often struck me that the more extraordinary a case at first appears the easier it is to button it up. The very peculiarity of it gives one something to work on. In simple affairs these don't occur, so it's harder to know where to start. Take this last business as a case in point. Certain factors stuck out a mile—call them clues if you like. To start with, both machines were stolen from training units. That might have been coincidence. On the other hand, the thief might have chosen them deliberately, knowing that training units usually have a variety of aircraft, and a large number of pupils and instructors who are always coming and going without having got to know each other very well. Thus, it would be possible for a stranger, provided he wore uniform or flying kit, to walk about without the slightest notice being taken of him. The public might not realise that, but an airman would, for which reason the thing looked to me from the start like the work of either a serving airman or someone who had been in the service and knew the routine. Such a man would know where everything was kept—tools, parachutes, and so on. He would know about meal-times, and know where to look for standing orders. Next, the two stations involved were close to each other, so the chances were that the thief lived in the same vicinity. Next, he himself could fly. He was, moreover, a pilot of some experience, since he could fly different types of service aircraft.

"All this boiled down to the probability of the thief being a serving officer or airman, or one recently discharged. The next point was the motive. Why did this fellow pinch the planes? He didn't want them. No man steals what he doesn't want. What did he want? The only thing missing was petrol. Not ordinary petrol, mark you. That could have been bought from any pump. Obviously that wouldn't do. It had to be high-octane aviation spirit, which is not available to the public. Very well. For what purpose could a man want aviation spirit? Obviously, for aviation. What sort of aviation?"

"Just a minute, old boy," put in Bertie. "He might have wanted the petrol to sell it. Petrol's worth money in the black market, don't forget."

"I don't forget it," answered Biggles. "Neither do I forget that if a man started selling aviation spirit to motorists he'd soon be caught. Someone would be bound to spot it and ask questions. An airman would certainly know the difference. Very well. Let's get on. A man doesn't steal a thing if he can get it by fair means. At any rate, he usually tries fair means first. The chances were, therefore, that our thief had tried to get aviation spirit through the proper channels, and had failed. To whom would he apply for a quota? Either to the Air Ministry or to the Ministry of Fuel and Power. An ex-airman would almost certainly apply to the Air Ministry, because he would have to explain the purpose for which it was required, and the Ministry would understand that. So, working on these lines of reasoning we arrive at the probability that the thief was an ex-R.A.F. officer, or a sergeant pilot, who for some purpose wanted a fairly big supply of aviation petrol.

"The next step was automatic. I rang up the Ministry of Civil Aviation and asked them to go through their records and let me have a list of people who, during the past twelve months, had applied for a quota of aviation spirit. There were four. Three, from newly-formed flying clubs, were granted. As they had got what they wanted they could be ruled out. The fourth applicant was an ex-sergeant pilot named Lutton who had been discharged on medical grounds. The application was declined, since the purpose for which the petrol was required did not, in the Air Ministry's view, justify it being granted. This, according to Lutton in his application form, was for the purpose of testing a new, ultra-light plane which he had designed and built. It was to be an air flivver—the cheap plane for the man in the street. As you know, the Air Ministry does not look kindly on private inventors, who are usually a danger, not only to themselves but to the general public. Moreover, there was another reason why the application was turned down. Lutton's service confidential reports revealed that he had been in trouble more than once. On one occasion he had tried to smuggle some watches into this country from Gibraltar. On another occasion he was put on a charge for the misuse of government tools and materials, which he had used for a private purpose. When I ascertained from his application form that this man lived in Norfolk, no great distance from the two airfields from which the planes had been stolen, I felt pretty sure that I was on the right track.

"The pattern of the thing now looked like this. Lutton's application for petrol had been turned down, but he was determined to get some. Putting on the uniform he still possessed he walked onto the tarmac of an R.A.F. station, took off in a Lysander and landed on his own field. Having withdrawn most of the petrol from the tanks, his problem was to dispose of the aircraft—not an easy matter in the ordinary way. What he did was put on a parachute, fly the machine to a lonely place on the Yorkshire moors, and step out. The plane crashed and he went home. It was all very easy. This petrol lasted him for a time, but when it was used up he simply repeated the performance. This time he was more careful and took a machine that would give him all the petrol he was ever likely to need—the Mosquito. Why he didn't use the parachute again I don't know. He may have damaged it in his last jump. Or he may not have felt like jumping again, particularly as it wasn't absolutely necessary. Anyway, to dispose of the aircraft he flew it to a big field some distance away, probably in the early hours of the morning, and left it there. That's how Lutton got his petrol.

"The rest you know. It was straightforward. I had the man's address. It was a farm, and, like most farms in that part of the country, had big flat fields. The outbuildings were fitted up as a workshop. He had got his petrol and was all set to carry on with his tests. Obviously his machine was ready to fly or he wouldn't have been in such a hurry to get the petrol. When I flew up this morning I was quite prepared for what I found. I went early because I reckoned that to be the time when he would do his testing. No one would be about and at dawn the air is usually still. What was more important to me, the dew is still on the grass, and any disturbance on it can be spotted at once from the air. When I saw wheel-tracks that faded out in the middle of a big field I knew that they could have been made only by one vehicle—an aircraft. I faked a forced landing so as not to alarm the man and went down to have a look round. That's all there was to it."

The telephone at Biggles's elbow rang. He picked up the receiver. "Yes, Bigglesworth here," he announced; and then, after listening for a minute, shook his head sadly. "Thank you, sir," he said, and hung up.

He looked at the others. "It seems that Lutton won't go to gaol after all," he murmured.

"Why not?" asked Ginger.

"Because when the police went to arrest him he tried to make a get-away in that home-made bird-cage which he called an aeroplane. At five hundred feet a wing came adrift and he went into the ground like a brick. He hadn't a hope. I told him the thing was a death-trap. Poor, silly fellow. Why will some chaps make such a mess of their lives?"